"You're perfec

Nash put his arm around her waist and did what he'd wanted to do since he'd first set eyes on her. He kissed her. Hard and sweet.

Behind him, Clover was standing in the doorway, her eyes narrowed thoughtfully. Oh, hell! What had she seen? Say something...anything....

"Is Nash going to be my new daddy?"

Stacey managed a laugh. "New daddy?" she repeated, unable to look at Nash.

"He was kissing you."

"Oh, yes, well, Nash was trying to cheer me up," she improvised.

Clover didn't look convinced. "When Sarah Graham's mummy was cheered up like that, Sarah had a new daddy *and* a new baby sister."

Oh, great. Stacey finally looked at Nash, hoping for a little assistance.

"Would you like a baby sister?" he asked Clover.

Born and raised in Berkshire, U.K., **Liz Fielding** started writing at the age of twelve, when she won a hymn-writing competition at her convent school. After a gap of more years than she is prepared to admit to, during which she worked as a secretary in Africa and the Middle East, got married and had two children, she was finally able to realize her ambition and turn to full-time writing in 1992.

She now lives with her husband, John, in West Wales, surrounded by mystical countryside and romantic crumbling castles, content to leave the traveling to her grown-up children and keeping in touch with the rest of the world via the Internet.

Look out for
The Bachelor's Baby
August 2001, #3666

Books by Liz Fielding

HARLEQUIN ROMANCE®
3570—AND MOTHER MAKES THREE
3618—HIS DESERT ROSE
3624—THE BEST MAN AND THE BRIDESMAID

HER IDEAL HUSBAND
Liz Fielding

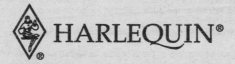

HARLEQUIN®

TORONTO • NEW YORK • LONDON
AMSTERDAM • PARIS • SYDNEY • HAMBURG
STOCKHOLM • ATHENS • TOKYO • MILAN • MADRID
PRAGUE • WARSAW • BUDAPEST • AUCKLAND

ISBN 0-373-03652-3

HER IDEAL HUSBAND

First North American Publication 2001.

CHAPTER ONE

NASH GALLAGHER knew he was crazy. He hadn't intended to stay. He was just passing through, stopping for a last look at the garden before the bulldozers moved in. Keeping a promise to an old man.

It had been a mistake.

Somehow he'd expected it to be the way it was in his memory. Everything ordered, everything perfect, the one place he had always been sure of in a confusing world.

Stupid.

Gardens weren't static things.

The walled kitchen garden might have survived the break-up of the estate, but the small garden centre his grandfather had run from it had been closed for nearly two years. Everything had run to seed, gone wild...

He dragged a hand over his face in a vain attempt to obliterate the image. He'd sworn he wouldn't fall for his grandfather's attempt at emotional blackmail, but maybe the old man knew him better than he knew himself.

It was the peach trees that did it.

Remembering how, when he was a boy, he'd been lifted up to pick the first ripe fruit, the taste of it, the juice running down his chin...

The memory was so strong that Nash rubbed his

chin against his shoulder, as if to wipe the juice away, then he angrily pulled away a handful of the weeds that crowded against an ancient trunk, choking it.

Stupid. In a few weeks it would all be gone.

But the old trees were covered with small fruit, swelling in the sudden burst of hot weather, refusing to give up despite the lack of pruning, despite the thick choking weeds at their roots. Like his grandfather, they refused to give up in the face of the inevitable. He couldn't leave them like that.

He wanted the men with the bulldozers to know they were smashing something that had once been cared for. It wouldn't take long. He could spare a day or two for the peach trees.

Except it wasn't just the peach trees.

There were the greenhouses with their old coke stoves and hot pipes. A wonderful place to play when it was too cold outside. A magic place full of warm, earthy scents.

It still was, despite the damage. A thin cat had given birth to a litter of kittens behind the stove. He'd spotted her once or twice, flashing through the long grass with some small creature clamped in her jaws and, as he stood there, the bravest of the kittens ventured out amongst the broken glass that littered the floor.

He moved it out of harm's way and then reached for an old broom. He was sweeping up the broken glass, wondering at how swift nature was to reclaim its own, when a ball blasted him out of the past as it smashed through the roof and he swore volubly as the fine shards showered him and sent the kitten flying back to safety of the nest.

For a moment he stared at the ball, big, bright red, intrusive, and an unexpected fury boiled up in him. People were so damned careless. Didn't they know, didn't they understand how long this had been here? Care about the generations of men who'd spent their lives working, harvesting, loving the place as he did?

He shook the glass out of his hair, carefully peeled off his T-shirt, then bent to pick up the ball, intent on telling the idiot who'd kicked it without a thought for the consequences, exactly what he thought of him.

'Mummy, Clover's kicked the ball over the wall again!'

At the most trying stage of refitting the handle to a freshly painted door, Stacey couldn't do much about her youngest daughter's plaintive cry, other than put her on hold.

'Tell her she'll have to wait,' she called back as she tried to juggle the handle and the screwdriver at the same time as fitting a screw with a life of its own into the hole. There were times, she felt, when two hands were simply not enough. But then, she had never been much use at this sort of thing.

Give her something solid to work with, a spade or a hoe, and she was perfectly at home. She could double-dig a vegetable plot, build a compost heap without raising a sweat. But put a screwdriver in her hand and she was all fingers and thumbs.

Not just a screwdriver. She wasn't much use with a paintbrush. There was more paint on her clothes and her skin than there was on the door.

'Mummy!'

'What?' The screw took advantage of this momentary distraction to make an escape bid. It hit the quarry-tiled floor, bounced once and disappeared beneath the dresser. Stacey only had four screws, the ones she'd taken out of the door plate when she'd removed it. Now she'd have to strip the dresser of china before she could move it and retrieve the wretched thing. Great. She dug screw number two out of her pocket, then remembered that her daughter wanted her for something. 'What is it, Rosie?'

'Nothing.' Then, 'Clover says not to worry, she'll climb over and get it herself.'

'Right,' she muttered, through teeth clamped around the handle of the screwdriver. If she could just get one wretched screw in place everything would be easier. She jammed it hard into the hole so that it stayed put while she retrieved the screwdriver and then realised what Rosie had said. *'No!'*

As she spun round to make sure she was obeyed, the metal plate pivoted on the screw and gouged an arc out of the freshly painted surface.

For a moment Stacey stared at the scarred paintwork, too shocked even to let slip the kind of word that mothers weren't supposed to know, let alone say.

Actually, she felt like screaming, but what would be the point? If she succumbed to the temptation to give in to her feelings and scream every time something went wrong, she would be permanently hoarse. Instead she dropped the screwdriver back into the toolbox, took a deep breath and, doing her best to keep calm, walked out into the garden.

It was not the end of the world, she told herself. She would get there one day. She would finish the kitchen. She would tile the bathroom. She would fix the guttering and decorate the dining room. She would do it because she had to. The house was unsellable the way it was. She'd tried it.

People might turn their noses up at twenty-year-old wallpaper, but there was the challenge to make a house over in their own image. Half-finished jobs just turned people off.

If only Mike had ever finished one thing before he'd started something else. But that had been Mike. There was always tomorrow. Except that he'd run out of tomorrows…

'Mummy! Clover's doing it!' Rosie's yell wrenched her from the beckoning arms of self-pity and she set off down the garden at a run.

Clover, nine years old and growing like a weed, had shimmied up the apple tree and was now dangling by her long skinny arms from the high brick wall that bordered the rear of the garden.

'Clover O'Neill, get down from there this minute!'

Clover glared at her younger sister, muttering something unappreciative at her, but she did as she was told, dropping from the wall and flattening a couple of foxgloves in the process.

'Sorry,' she said, trying to straighten them.

Stacey just sighed, picked the flower stems and firmed the ground around the plants. The advantage of growing what most of her neighbours sniffily considered to be weeds was that they could take pretty much everything that two lively children could throw at them. 'What on earth do you think you were doing up there?'

'You said not to disturb you while you were fixing the door, so I was going to get the ball myself.' She said this as if it was the most reasonable thing in the world. Clover could have won Olympic gold for 'reason'.

'Well, that's very thoughtful of you, sweetheart, but I'd have been a lot more disturbed by a broken leg,' she reasoned right back, firmly suppressing a shudder. The wall was a couple of hundred years old at least and in some places it was held together by little more than the mossy stonecrop that clung to it. 'You are never—I repeat, never—to climb on that wall. It's dangerous.' Her daughter rolled her eyes, dramatically. 'I mean it!'

'But how are we going to get our ball back?' Rosie asked.

Clover glared at her little sister. 'If you'd kept your mouth shut, we'd have it back now.'

'That's enough. Both of you. You'll get your ball.' They'd get it the same way they always did. She would climb over when they weren't around to see the bad example she was setting them. 'I'm sure someone will see it and throw it back. They did last time.'

'But that could take for ever,' Rosie protested. 'No one goes in there any more, not since it closed.'

It was true that the garden centre that backed onto their garden was rapidly turning into a wilderness since ill-health had forced Archie Baldwin, the old guy that ran it, to retire a couple of years earlier.

She must find time to go and visit him again soon, she thought guiltily. He'd taught her so much. The least she could do was take him a tin of shortbread, tell him all the latest gossip from the village. And maybe ask him about the depressing rumour going round the neighbourhood that he'd sold the land to a developer.

It would be a lot easier to sell her house if the views could be described as rural.

Attractive detached Victorian cottage-style property in village setting with scope for improvement. Interesting wild flower garden.

It sounded appealing. Until you saw it and understood exactly what 'scope for improvement' meant. How much money it would take. And, as her sister was fond of pointing out, most people tried to eradicate buttercups and daisies from their borders.

But the garden really wasn't the problem. It was the house. The estate agent she'd asked to value the place hadn't pulled any punches. The house needed some serious attention if it was going to make anywhere near the price it should and a housing estate blocking the view was not going to help. Or light industrial units. Maybe she should stop worrying about her precious wild flowers and plant a fast-growing hedge right now…

'Mum!'

She let go of future worries and returned to the immediate one. 'I'm sorry, Clover, but you shouldn't have kicked your ball over there in the first place.'

'You can't play football without kicking,' Clover pointed out, but kindly, as if to someone who wasn't expected to understand. 'Come on, Rosie. Mummy'll get it for us; she always does. She just doesn't want us to see *her* climbing over the—' she made a sign like quotation marks '—great big dangerous wall.'

'Clover O'Neill, that's—'

'It's no use pretending, Mummy. I saw you last time.'

Stacey was not above circumventing the truth in a good cause, but there was no point in perjuring herself to no purpose, so she didn't deny it, contenting herself with a firm, 'You were supposed to have been in bed.'

'I saw you from the bathroom window,' Clover said, cheekily, and grinned. 'You will get it, won't you? Now?'

Since she'd been caught out, there seemed little point in waiting until the girls were in bed. 'All right. But I mean it. You are not to do this yourself, ever. Promise?'

'I promise.' And Clover solemnly drew a cross over her heart. Just the way Mike used to when he promised he'd fix something tomorrow. Just the way he used to promise he'd take care when he went out on his motorbike...

Stacey swallowed. 'Okay.' She dropped the flowers, then approached the wall, jumped and grabbed the top, pulling herself smoothly up to sit astride the crumbling brickwork.

The derelict garden centre had once been the walled kitchen garden of a grand house that had long since been turned into the headquarters of some multi-national corporation.

From the top, she could see the south wall and the ancient espaliered peach trees. There were a couple of big old greenhouses that had lost a fair amount of glass in a bad storm. Until then, she'd used them to raise her own seedlings. Well, Archie had told her to help herself.

Now it all looked so sad, grown wild with frightening speed and run to a riot of weeds that were beginning to flower in the gravel paths and between great clumps of perennials that had burst out of plastic pots and made themselves at home.

She glanced back down at the girls. 'Stay there and don't move,' she said, then jumped down into a mini-meadow of buttercups and dog daisies and began to look about her for the girls' ball.

It was big and red and should have been easy enough to find. The trouble was, she kept getting distracted. First by a clump of poppies with scarlet silken petals. Great. She'd come back for some seeds later in the summer. If she was still there later in the summer. Maybe she would have sold the house by then. Or maybe not.

It was a depressing thought either way.

She stopped to look at a huge blousy peony. Not

her kind of flower but it broke her heart to think of it being torn up by a bulldozer. Even if she lifted it, though, it probably wouldn't survive. Peonies hated to be moved. They had her sympathy. She didn't want to move, either. She was comfortable where she was and she'd put down long roots, but, like the peonies, she didn't have a choice.

At least in her case the move wouldn't be fatal. Just very painful. And the end of any chance of getting her own wild plant nursery up and running.

She pushed her way along the overgrown paths, looking for the ball and wondering just how far it could have gone, when she caught a glimpse of red beyond a row of overgrown bushes. She pushed through and saw the strawberries. Big and red and luscious.

Nash emerged from the greenhouse and looked around. Nothing. No one. Then at the far side of the garden he saw someone peering over. It was a child. A little girl. Then she disappeared and his anger evaporated with her.

She meant no harm. It was an accident. The place was a wreck and she could hardly make it worse. He began to pick his way around the raised beds, the thicket of waist-high weeds, planning on tossing the ball back over the wall.

He was about halfway there when another, much older girl appeared, her baggy shorts giving him ample opportunity to admire her long legs as she flung them over the wall. Not a little girl, this one, not if the skimpy top she was filling out so nicely was anything to go by. And he found himself grinning as she jumped down to wade through the knee-high flowers, the sun backlighting the strands of chestnut hair that had escaped the little bobble thing she'd used to hold it back from her face.

She was too busy checking the ground to notice him and he remained quite still, watching her as she waded through the long grass looking about her for the ball. Every now and then she would stop to look at a flower. Not picking it, but just looking, gently touching the petals of the big daisies, the vivid poppies as if saying hello.

Definitely not a vandal.

Then, as she stopped by one of the peonies, the sun lit up her face and he saw a look of genuine pleasure lift the corner of her mouth, before her smile faded to sadness. She wasn't a girl at all, he realised, but a full-grown woman.

He took half a step, opened his mouth to call out to her, but she turned suddenly. And he knew she'd spotted the strawberries.

It would be a criminal waste to leave them to the slugs, Stacey thought. The wretched creatures already feasted like kings in her garden, despite all her environmentally friendly attempts at controlling them. It was only fair to share, she reasoned, as she got down on her hands and knees and picked half a dozen of the biggest strawberries she could find as a treat for Clover and Rosie.

Then she picked one for herself and ate it warm from the sun, the way strawberries should be eaten.

The juice dribbled down her chin and she wiped it off with her fingers and then licked them. Heaven. She couldn't think how the slugs, or the birds, had missed them, but she was glad they had and took one more.

In fact, if the garden was going to be bulldozed for housing, she might as well come back when Clover and Rosie were at school and get some runners; then they could have their own strawberries next year. She checked to see how soon the little plantlets would be ready. Then she stopped.

What was the point? They wouldn't be there next year.

Okay, so she'd been saying that for the last two years, but time was running out. She might not be saddled with a mortgage, but there was no chance that she could sell enough wild plants to keep up with the outgoings. And if she was reduced to producing boxes of petunias and bizzie lizzies, she might as well get a job in an office. And with that miserable thought, she began to back out of the strawberry bed.

Her feet encountered an obstruction and she stopped, frowning. She hadn't noticed anything on the path as she'd crawled in amongst the strawberries and, puzzled, she turned to look behind her.

The obstruction was wearing a pair of well-worn boots with thick socks rolled down over them. Above the boots were two long, well-muscled legs with scarred brown knees, hairy thighs and a pair of denim cut-offs, worn duster-soft with use, clinging to the kind of hips that should be carrying a health warning.

'Can I help?' The voice that went with the legs was duster-soft, too.

Stacey felt her face turn the colour of the poppies. To be caught trespassing was bad enough. To have a handful of filched strawberries as evidence of her fall from grace rang a loud nine on the Richter scale of embarrassment; yet to abandon them would only compound her crime. She was still trying to think of something to say when Clover rescued her.

'Mummee! Have you found it yet?' Her oldest daughter, paying technical lip-service to her promise not to climb the old wall, was instead perched on a branch of an equally ancient apple tree and peering anxiously over the wall.

'Get down!' She should have been angry, but her daughter's appearance at least lent her the cloak of respectability. She was a mother. A widowed mother, moreover. What could be more respectable than that?

She scrambled to her feet and, turning to face her embarrassment head on, found herself looking up at the kind of man who should not only have a health warning tattooed to his backside, but to his chest, his arms and his thoroughly workmanlike shoulders. To say nothing of a lean, tanned face, periwinkle-blue eyes and the kind of floppy sun-bleached hair that had always gone straight to her knees. Which was why she'd been married on her eighteenth birthday and a mother by her nineteenth, sieving vegetables for baby Clover instead of learning the business aspects of growing them at the local agricultural college.

That this delectable hunk of manhood didn't have a health warning tattooed to his limbs or any other part of him, she could see for herself since, except for a suntan, the cut-offs were all that he was wearing. Apart from the boots and socks. And she had no doubt that his feet and ankles matched the rest of him and were of the killer variety. Like his smile.

'Is this what you were looking for?'

'Looking for? Oh, looking for…' Stacey made a determined effort to drag her chin out of the strawberry bed and get her knees under control. 'Er, yes.'

'I was in one of the greenhouses over there when it came through the roof.' He tossed the football, spun it on one finger, then caught it, balancing it on the palm of his hand. 'That's quite a kick.' His glance measured the distance from the broken panes of the greenhouse roof to the top of the wall. 'For a girl.' And he grinned up at Clover, who was still clinging to her tree top perch. 'Is your dad a professional coach?'

'No, my daddy's in heaven.'

Well, as conversation-stoppers went, that took some beating. 'Clover, if you don't get down right now,' Stacey warned, turning away from the disturbing sight of the man's muscle-packed shoulders, 'I'll leave your ball over here.' Mike had had shoulders like that. All brawn and no brain, her sister had said. Dee had always been the smart one.

While she never learned.

Clover disappeared.

'I bet she's a handful.'

'Oh, no, not really. Just football-mad.' Other women had dainty little girls who yearned for satin pointe shoes and a starring role at the Royal Ballet. She was usually torn between pride and mortification that her first-born had ball skills that put the boys at her primary school to shame and whose most ardent yearning concerned a pair of football boots way beyond the means of the widow's mite. His teasing 'For a girl…' brought her firmly down on the pride side, for once. 'She's captain of the school team.' Then, 'Was there much damage?'

'Damage?' He needed prompting, too, it seemed. 'To the greenhouse.'

'I don't think one pane more or less will be noticed, do you?' The grin softened into a smile.

'N-no, I suppose not…' she stuttered. A smile like that should be licenced. Then, 'Oh, Lord, you weren't…I mean…' No, of course he wasn't hurt. She could see for herself that his golden skin was unblemished. Well, apart from the faint white line of an old scar across his collarbone.

Then she saw the sun glint off a shard of glass clinging to his hair and without thinking she reached up and picked it off.

CHAPTER TWO

STACEY stared at the sharp sliver of glass she was holding between her fingers and felt herself go hot all over.

She couldn't believe she had done that. What on earth was she going to do now?

Despite the fact that she was totally unable to meet his eyes, the hunk seemed to understand her predicament because he dropped the ball and, grasping her wrist to steady a hand that was unaccountably shaking, carefully extracted the sliver of glass from between her fingers. Then he dropped it on the path and ground it to powder beneath his heel.

'Thanks.' Her voice was shaking as much as her wrist had done.

'I think I'm the one who should be thanking you.' He was still holding her wrist, his long fingers circling it, heating it, melting the bones. For a long moment he kept her his prisoner before suddenly dropping it as if he too were burning, raking his fingers through his hair as if needing to keep them occupied. Then he looked at his hand. 'See, I'm always doing that. I could have got a nasty cut.'

She shrugged, awkwardly. 'It's being a mother,' she began. 'You just can't help yourself.' She swallowed, and tried to ignore the dangerous tingle where his fingers had touched her wrist. She wasn't

20

feeling motherly. Oh, no. Not one bit. 'I, um, helped myself to a few strawberries,' she said, bringing up the subject before he did. 'I hope you don't mind.'

'I thought you were very restrained not to take more. Were they good?' He'd been standing there watching her? Her face competed with the poppies again.

'Mummee!' Another desperate plea.

'I think the captain of the team wants to get on with the game,' he said, stooping to pick up the ball, offering it to her.

'What? Oh, no, that's Rosie. She's only seven. Clover makes her play in goal. She's not very good.' She took the ball, tucking it under her arm. 'I'll try to keep them under control, but when they've been in school all day…'

'No problem. I'll be around for a day or two. If the ball comes over again, just give me a shout and I'll throw it back.'

'You could be sorry you said that.' She forced her legs to make a move, to put some distance between her and the temptation to stay and just look at him, but he walked alongside her as she headed back to the wall.

Was he going to offer her a hand up? She tried not to think about his hands around her waist, his breath on her neck.

'What's going to happen to this place?' she asked quickly. To distract herself. 'Do you know?' She looked back. 'I heard it was going to be sold to some awful developer.' He didn't say anything. 'Oh, Lord, is that you?'

'Would that be a problem?' The corner of his mouth tugged up into a smile as he glanced sideways at her.

She wished she'd done more than tie her hair back with one of the girls' bobbles. And put on some mascara. Lipstick even.

To paint a door? Get real, Stacey; this guy is a Grade A hunk and you're a mother of two with the muscle-tone to prove it...

'We'd miss the view,' she said, quickly. Not that it would be hers for long. One wild-flower meadow at the local primary school, no matter how much admired, did not a career make. She really had to stop kidding herself that she could make a business out of her passion for wild flowers and get the house into shape so that she could sell it. He glanced across the garden to the fields rising away to the hazy hills in the distance. 'Maybe they won't get planning permission,' she said, hopefully.

'They already have.'

'Oh.' She'd expected it, but it was still a blow. 'Houses?' she asked hopefully.

'Industrial units.'

'Oh,' she repeated dully. Then, 'Are you working for the developers?'

He shook his head. 'Just for myself. Nash Gallagher,' he said, introducing himself, stopping to offer his hand before realising that, between the strawberries and the ball, her hands were now fully occupied. It was probably just as well. She hadn't recovered from the hand around the wrist yet. Palm to palm was going to leave her reeling. And incapable of climbing that wretched wall.

But she could hardly deny him her name. 'Stacey O'Neill. And you've probably gathered that the nuisances are Clover and Rosie.'

'Well, I'm glad to have met you. As I said, I'll be staying here for a few days, in case you see a light and think someone might be up to no good and call the police.'

'Staying? You mean you're camping? Here?' She looked around, saw the small one-man tent pitched in a shady corner and wondered if he had permission. Then decided that it was none of her business.

'This is the height of luxury compared to some of the places I've lived,' he assured her, evidently mistaking her concern. 'It's got running water, plumbing—'

She wanted to ask what places, but restrained herself and wondered if he'd broken into the office to get at the plumbing and running water. Did it matter? If it was all going to be flattened... 'You're still sleeping in a tent.' Then she shrugged. 'I suppose it's okay when it's not raining.' It had been a very wet spring.

'Are you suggesting this spell of good weather is unlikely to last?' he asked, with just a touch of irony in his voice to match the infinitesimal lift of one eyebrow.

'This good weather has lasted all of a week so far, which, for this summer, is a record.' Then she relented. 'But according to the forecast you should be safe for a day or two.'

He glanced up at the cloudless sky for a moment. 'Let's hope so.'

'Mummeeeeee!'

'They're getting impatient.' She tossed the ball over the wall. 'I'll try to keep it on our side of wall from now on.'

'It's not a problem, really.'

Maybe not, but she had one. Getting over the wall with what remained of her dignity intact while he stood there and looked at her winter-white legs. Winter-white splashed with the forget-me-not-blue gloss that she'd finished the door with. And a scraping of brick dust. And squishy green plant juice on her knees from her expedition into the strawberry bed.

She looked at the strawberries in her hand and wished she left them for the slugs. Now she would have to get over the wall with one hand, or throw them away.

'Can I help?' he offered. Again.

She thought about those big hands lifting her, or giving her a push from behind. 'Er…' This was getting ridiculous. She was heading at what seemed like break-neck speed towards thirty. She had two children. Blushing was for girls… 'Perhaps if you hold the strawberries while I climb up?' she suggested.

He made no move to take them; instead he linked his hands together and offered them as a foothold. She felt a momentary stab of disappointment, then quickly placed her battered tennis shoe into the cup of his palms, and as he lifted her, she grabbed for the wall and was deposited on the top without the usual ungainly knee-skinning scramble.

'Thanks,' she said.

'My pleasure,' he replied, grinning broadly as she swung her legs over to the other side. 'Drop in any time.'

She pretended not to hear, sliding down into her own garden and finishing off the foxgloves in her hurry. And not doing the strawberries much good, either. Despite the lift over the wall, she had still managed to squash them into a juicy mush.

Nash Gallagher watched as his new neighbour swung her lovely legs over the wall and quickly disappeared. She'd been decorating, he'd noticed. There were streaks of blue paint on her thighs and clothes and her fingers, as she'd cupped the strawberries protectively in her hand, still had paint embedded around her nails. Did she just enjoy doing it herself?

With Daddy in heaven, it would seem she had little choice.

Stacey was mashing the strawberries to mix with ice cream for Clover and Rosie's tea when the abandoned door handle, still dangling by one partly driven screw, gave up the unequal struggle with gravity and fell noisily to the floor.

Clover, finishing off her baked beans, glanced at it. Then she said, 'What this house needs is a capable man.' Stacey took her plate and replaced it with the ice cream. 'Or one with plenty of money.'

'Clover!'

'It's true,' Rosie added, helpfully. 'Aunt Dee said so.'

Dee was undoubtedly right, but she wished her sister would keep her thoughts to herself. Or at least not voice them in front of the girls.

Fat chance. Her sister was hell-bent on fixing her up with a new husband, someone who fitted Dee's idea of what was suitable for a little sister who couldn't be trusted to choose someone for herself. Someone steady. Someone who wouldn't, under any circumstances, ride a motorcycle.

An accountant, perhaps. Or, even better, an actuary, like her own husband. A man genetically programmed not to take unacceptable risks.

Unfortunately, much as she liked her brother-in-law, Stacey just couldn't get terribly excited at the thought of being married to his clone. Her thoughts strayed to the stranger camping on the far side of her garden and she found herself smiling. There were some things that money couldn't ever compensate for.

But as Stacey handed her younger daughter her ice cream, she promised herself she would have that door repainted, with its furniture in place and working when her sister came to lunch on Saturday. If it killed her.

Actually, though, her encounter with Nash Gallagher had given her an idea. Well, more than one, but she was a realist. Sex among the strawberries was fine when you were young and fancy-free but mothers had responsibilities. Mothers had to be sensible.

She let the tempting thought slip away and concentrated on the sensible one. Her house might not be fit for a feature in one of those 'beautiful homes' magazines, and it might not appeal to fussy buyers with a world of houses to choose from, but it was habitable. And she had a spare bedroom. Two, if she included the attic. Nash might be happy to sleep in a tent, but there were plenty of other people who would rather have hot water and clean sheets. Maybe she could let the rooms to a couple of students.

At her present rate of progress it would be a while before she could lick the house into shape and two students would make quite a difference when it came to paying the bills. And if they were a couple of willing lads, or girls, the kind who knew one end of a screwdriver from the other, it would be even better. In return for a little home cooking, they might achieve the same purpose as a capable man without all the disadvantages that went with the kind of husband a widow approaching thirty, with two little girls to bring up, could hope to attract.

Nash found himself grinning as he cleared away the broken glass, smiling as he remembered the way Stacey had coloured up when he'd caught her with her hand in the strawberry patch. He'd have sworn modern women had forgotten how to blush.

He should be feeling guilty for embarrassing her like that: a young widow with two little girls.

Thoroughly ashamed of himself. Hell, he was ashamed, but that blush had been worth it.

Then the smile faded as he looked about him.

Industrial units.

Landscaped, low-rise industrial units. On paper it hadn't sounded so bad. Standing here with the gentle slope of the wheatfield rising to a spinney that broke up the smooth line of the earth against the sky and with the peach trees basking against the centuries-old wall, it wasn't quite so easy to be dismissive of the destruction.

On paper the choice had looked simple. Putting down roots had no appeal to him. He wasn't sentimental about the past. His childhood hadn't been the kind to get sentimental over.

But standing there, surrounded by the few good memories, it wasn't quite so easy to dismiss.

'You're not getting any younger and children are a high-cost luxury.'

'Make a record, Dee; it'll save the wear and tear on your vocal cords,' Stacey said, without rancour. She knew her sister meant well.

'I would if I thought you'd listen to it. You need a husband and the girls need a father.'

'I don't need a husband, I need an odd-job man. And the girls have a father. No one can replace Mike.'

'No.' Dee, apparently about to make an unflattering comment about his parenting skills, hesitated, and went for tact instead. 'Mike's not here, Stacey,' she said, kindly. Tact? Kindly? This was more than her usual 'it's-time-you-moved-on' speech. She was up to something, Stacey thought. 'You owe it to them to find them a father…a father-figure,' she amended, quickly. 'Someone who could give them all the advantages they deserve.' Stacey began clearing the table in an attempt to avoid what was coming next. Dee was not to be distracted. 'Lawrence Fordham for instance.'

So, this wasn't just a general buck-yourself-up-and-get-out-there pep-talk. This was altogether more serious.

'Lawrence?' she repeated. 'You want me to marry your boss?'

'Why not? He's a nice man. Steady, reliable, mature.' Adjectives that could, by no stretch of the imagination, have been applied to Mike. But then, at eighteen, Stacey hadn't been looking for those qualities in a man. Which was just as well, since she hadn't got them. 'He's just a bit shy, that's all.'

'Just a bit,' she agreed. She'd been put next to him at a recent lunch party at her sister's house… Ah. So that was it. She wouldn't make an effort, so her sister was making it for her. It should have been funny. But once Dee got an idea in her head she was harder to shake off than a shadow. 'Small talk drips from his lips the way blood drips from a stone.'

'That's not fair. Once you get to know him—'

'I do know him and you're right, he's a nice man.' If you enjoyed talking about cheese production, or yoghurt culture. 'I just wasn't planning on anything more intimate—'

'Okay, he's not pin-up material, but let's face it, sweetie, how many men-to-die-for do you know who are lining up, panting for a date?'

'He's panting?' Stacey enquired, wickedly. 'Lawrence?'

'Of course not,' Dee snapped. 'You know what I mean!' Stacey knew. She'd had her man-to-die-for and there was only one of those per lifetime. Which was probably just as well. Now she had to be sensible, but the prospect of dating men like Lawrence for the rest of her life, or worse, settling down with someone like him, was just so depressing.

'He's solid, Stacey. He wouldn't let you down.'

Meaning that if he was inconsiderate enough to die on her, he wouldn't leave her with a house that swallowed money, two children to bring up single-handed and no visible means of support, Stacey supposed.

'He couldn't let me down, Dee. We are acquaintances. Nothing more,' she added, just to make her position quite clear.

'Well, that's about to change,' Dee replied, ignoring her sister's position. 'I told him that you'd be his date for the firm's dinner next Saturday.'

'You did what!' Stacey didn't wait for her sister for repeat herself. 'You've got to be kidding!'

'Why? He's personable. He's got all his own hair and teeth and no bad habits.' Stacey wondered if her sister was prepared to guarantee that in writing, but didn't want to prolong the conversation. 'He'll make someone a wonderful husband and you need one more than most.'

'Husband? I thought we were just talking about a date.'

'We are. But you're mature people. You'd be good for Lawrence, bring him out of himself. And he'd be very good for you. He wouldn't even mind if you turned his garden into a weed patch.' Because he wouldn't notice. 'You do the best you can, but don't pretend it isn't a struggle.' Stacey wasn't about to. It wouldn't make a bit of difference if she did, because Dee knew better. 'You will come on Saturday, won't you?'

'Oh, Dee…'

'Please.' Please? She was that desperate? 'I'll promise not to mention the subject again for a whole month if you do,' she promised.

'Good grief, I'm almost tempted. But I haven't got a thing to wear,' Stacey said, falling back on the age-old excuse.

'You can wear my black dress.'

'Your black dress?' She should have known that her sister had a fall-back plan to cover her fall-back plan… Then her jaw dropped. 'You don't mean *the* black dress?'

'Of course I mean *the* black dress,' Dee said, calmly, and Stacey finally managed a laugh.

'Now I'm really worried. Tell me, have you got some enormous bonus riding on your ability to fix Lawrence up with a date for this dinner?'

Dee's brows quirked invitingly. 'Would you go out with him if I had?'

'Would you split it with me?' Then, quickly, 'Don't answer that. I don't want to be that tempted.'

'Oh, come on, Stacey. It's a night out. Gorgeous restaurant, lovely food, rich bloke. How many offers like that do you get these days?' Not many. Actually, none. 'He's completely house-trained, I promise you.' Dee meant to reassure her, but Stacey didn't want a house-trained man. What she wanted was someone like Nash Gallagher. All right, not *like* Nash Gallagher. She wanted him. In person. 'You'll be safe enough,' she promised. 'Tim and I will be there.'

That'd be fun. An evening with Mr Nice, Mrs Bossy and Mr Deadly-Dull-but-Totally-Dependable…

But Stacey caught a tantalising glimpse of a way out. 'If you're going to the dinner, I won't have anyone to babysit.' There were many times when she wished her parents hadn't sold up their business and moved to Spain to grow old disgracefully in the sun. This was not one of them. And Vera, her next-door neighbour and best friend, who looked after the girls on her occasional—very occasional—evening out, worked on Saturday nights at the local petrol station.

'Clover and Rosie can stay over at our house,' Dee replied, with all the firmness of a woman who'd made it in business and wasn't about to take no for an answer. Even from her tiresome little sister. 'Ingrid is looking forward to having them.' The firmness of a woman who'd made it to the top in business and the smugness of one who'd got a 'treasure' for an au pair. 'And I'm going to take you for a facial and a manicure, too.'

'Now that is tempting,' Stacey said. She glanced at her hands and surreptitiously scraped away the rim of blue paint that was stubbornly clinging to her thumb-nail. Her sister had bought her some horrendously expensive gardener's handcream a while back; maybe she should start using it. And maybe Dee was right. After all her hard work, she deserved a treat.

A meal she hadn't had to cook herself, a manicure and a chance to wear a designer label frock certainly came under that heading.

'Can I really borrow your black dress?'

'I'll bring it round tomorrow.'

'Heavens, Dee, the dinner isn't until next Saturday…'

She grinned. 'I know. More than enough time for you to come up with a dozen excuses, but once that dress is in your wardrobe you won't be able to resist the chance to wear it.'

'That's sneaky.' But maybe she could put it on, do the whole mascara bit and get Clover to kick her ball over the wall… Dee's voice dragged her back from dreamland.

'If sneaky is what it takes to get you out of the house, I'll go as low as it takes.' And she grinned. 'Can you spare some more of those strawberries, or are you saving them for the girls?' She glanced out to where Clover and Rosie were sitting in the long grass, picking daisies and decorating their young cousin, Harry, with daisy chains.

'Finish them off. They've had more than enough.'

Dee scooped the fruit into her bowl. 'They're the best I've tasted this year. Where did you get them?'

'Um…from a neighbour.' And Stacey felt herself blush. She hadn't seen Nash since the afternoon she'd climbed the wall and been caught with her fingers in the strawberry patch. Only the glow of a camp fire late at night when she'd been going to bed.

And she'd been congratulating herself on resolutely sticking to her guns and refusing to ask Nash to look for the ball when Clover kicked it over the wall just before bedtime, no matter how much her daughter had pleaded. Of course, she hadn't had the promise of an Armani dress, then.

No, she was determined. She wasn't looking for Mr Right. And she had had enough experience of Mr Wrong to last a lifetime. The girls would have to wait until he noticed it. And if he took his time about it, maybe Clover would learn to be more careful.

He didn't, of course.

Clover had found the football in a carrier hooked over a branch of the apple tree first thing that morning. And resting on top of the football had been a large chip punnet full of strawberries.

Dee's eyes narrowed. 'A neighbour? What neighbour?' Her sister's scrutiny only made things worse. 'I thought you were the one who handed out all the garden goodies around here.' Then, 'Are you blushing?'

Stacey covered her cheeks with her hands. 'Don't be silly, it's just the heat,' she said, quickly. 'And I've been thinking…'

'Thinking?' Dee raised her brows.

'I've been thinking,' Stacey repeated, ignoring her sister's sarcastic response, 'about letting out one of my rooms to a student. What do you think?'

Stacey knew exactly what her sister would think, but she needed to change the subject, fast.

'I think you should put the house on the market and sell it for whatever you can get while the sun's shining. With luck prospective buyers will be so busy reminiscing about the last time they saw a dog rose, they won't notice that the paintwork's peeling and the gutters are falling apart.' She paused. 'Cutting the grass might help.'

'If I took in a couple of students,' Stacey said, ignoring the sarcasm, 'my financial circumstances would improve, I would be able to get the house into shape and then, if I decide to sell...when,' she amended, quickly, before Dee could launch forth on the subject, 'when I sell, I'll get a better price.'

'You've been saying that since Mike died.'

'I know. But there's a lot to do.'

'I won't argue with that.' Then she shrugged. 'All right, I'm through nagging for today.' She stood up. 'I think you're mad, but we might as well have a look at what you've got to offer.'

Dee was shaking her head over the lack of tiling in the bathroom when Stacey saw Nash on the far side of the wall. He was shifting a heavy wheelbarrow full of rubbish in the direction of a faint curl of smoke; the sun glinting off his sweat-slicked skin, the hard curve of well-developed biceps. As if he'd felt her gaze on him he turned, looked up and their eyes seemed to lock...

'Actually, you've got a point,' she said, quickly, easing her sister out of the bathroom. She knew exactly what Dee would have to say about Nash Gallagher. He was temptation on legs and she'd fallen once before. 'I always take care about splashing, but I can't expect anyone else to bother.' She threw one last, lingering glance out of the window. 'I'll see to it. Will you put a card on the notice board at the university for me on the way home?'

'If you insist. Maybe you should put a card up in the village shop, too. Or even an ad in the paper. Or...' Dee remembered that she had other plans for Stacey.

'Or marry Lawrence and never worry about money again?' Dee didn't deny it. 'What makes you think he'd want to marry me? I'm hardly a prize catch for a man in his position. Even supposing I'd consider marrying a man for his money.' Her sister, infuriatingly, just smiled, and it occurred to Stacey that she wasn't the only one being set up. She might actually have felt some sympathy with Lawrence as a fellow victim of her sister's matchmaking plans, but he was safe enough from her. Besides, she had problems of her own.

Such as what Nash Gallagher would make of the tin of home-made shortbread that Clover had taken it upon herself to leave on top of the wall as a thank-you present for returning her football. The shortbread she'd made for Archie.

By the time she'd discovered it was missing and Clover had admitted what she'd done, it was too late to do anything about it. It had gone.

CHAPTER THREE

'HAVE you heard what's happening to the old garden centre, yet?' Dee asked, as they walked towards her expensive new Italian car.

Unwilling to admit to the industrial units—she'd had enough nagging for one day—Stacey just said, 'There's someone working over there, clearing the place up.'

'They must have got planning permission, then.' Dee sighed and shook her head. 'I did warn you. The house will be worth nothing if you don't sell it quickly.'

'If I could have sold quickly, I would have done.'

'No, darling, you wouldn't. You've been putting off the inevitable, hoping your numbers will come up on the lottery so you don't have to move at all.'

'Not true. I can't afford lottery tickets.'

Dee looked startled. 'Are things that bad? Look, please...'

'Don't!'

'All right, all right,' she said, quickly backing off from offering money. 'But you know what I mean. You don't want to move. All this fiddling about trying to fix up Mike's do-it-yourself disasters is just your way of putting off the inevitable. Let it go, Stacey. Let it go...'

Stacey picked up her two-year-old nephew and

began to fasten him into his car seat, pretending she hadn't heard. 'Okay, Harry?' Harry grinned at her. 'You are so gorgeous, sweetheart.' She straightened and stepped back. 'I wish I had a little boy just like you.'

'Feeling broody?' Dee asked, slyly. She hadn't been… 'Marry Lawrence and I'm sure he'll oblige.'

'Really? Does it have to be a permanent arrangement? I'd be perfectly happy with just the baby.'

'As if you didn't have enough troubles.' But her sister was wearing a suspiciously smug little smile, no doubt counting on Stacey's hormones to do the dirty work for her. 'I'll call round with the dress.'

'Fine.'

'You won't cry off at the last moment, will you?'

'Don't nag. I can't promise to make Lawrence's night but—' she paused as Dee's helpful suggestion that the children stay over at her house with Harry, in the care of the doting Ingrid, suddenly acquired a less innocent interpretation; there was no such thing as a free babysitter '—but I won't let you down.' She would be making her own babysitting arrangements, though. 'You won't forget to put up a notice about the room, will you?'

'You're quite sure you want to do this? You might get the tenant from hell.'

'As long as he can pay the rent, I don't mind where he comes from.'

Stacey watched her sister drive away, not entirely sure she could trust Dee to put up the 'Room to Let' notice for her. Her sister had an entirely different agenda, wanting her safely married to someone who would pay to send the girls to a private school and install them all in a house with every modern convenience, a house where the shelves had been put up by a proper carpenter—or at least someone who knew how to use a level.

She meant well.

Stacey turned and looked at her home with its sharply pointed gables and piecrust bargeboarding. She loved it, but she had to admit that it could have been the prototype for the 'crooked little house'.

It had been, in that favourite estate agents' phrase, 'in need of improvement' when Mike had inherited it from his uncle. Unfortunately, he was not the man for the job.

Mike had only ever been good at one thing. A husband, a father, needed more than five stars in the good sex guide...

'What are you looking at, Mummy?'

Stacey dragged herself back to the present. 'There are some housemartins.' She stooped down to Rosie's level. 'Look, they've built a house under the eaves. Can you see?'

'Wow, that's so cool.'

'Yes, isn't it? If they raise a family there, they'll come back every year.' Not quite paying guests, but just as welcome. 'Run and fetch Clover, will you, sweetheart? I want to walk down to the village.' Just in case Dee decided not to risk the chance of her plans being upset by a student needing a room this late in the college year, Stacey would put a card in the window of the village shop. Before she lost her nerve.

And when they got back, she'd cut the lawn. Well, trim the heads off the daisies, at any rate, which was all her lawn mower was capable of. University students probably wouldn't notice, but she didn't want to risk putting anyone off.

Dear Nash

Mummy says I have to wait until you find my ball, but that mite be forever if you don't know I've lost it. So I'm just telling you I kicked it over the wall again. Sorry. Love, Clover

PS Please don't tell Mummy I rote this. I'm supposed to be pashunt and wait.

Nash spotted the note, stuck in a crack at the top of the wall, when he emerged from his tent at first light. The football took a while to find, but he didn't mind that. He'd been looking for an opportunity to further his acquaintance with Stacey O'Neill. He'd hoped the strawberries would do the trick.

She hadn't responded in person, but the tin of shortbread suggested he wouldn't be rebuffed if he looked over the wall to say thanks. The sound of a very sick lawn mower was all the excuse he needed.

Stacey was crouched over the mower, feeding its apparently bottomless thirst for oil, when something made her look up. Nash Gallagher was sitting on top of the wall, watching her, his incredible legs just waiting for a invitation to jump down and make themselves at home.

'Need a hand?' he said.

'What I need is a new lawn mower,' she said, standing up, her face flushed from bending over the ancient machine. Maybe. 'I just hope I've got enough oil to keep it going until I've finished.' The fact that the grass was six inches high wasn't exactly helping.

He jumped down without waiting for the invitation and gave the mower an exploratory push, then frowned. 'Have you got a spanner?'

'Well, um, yes.' He waited. 'You want me to fetch it?'

'It might be a good idea. Unless it's trained to come when you whistle?' One corner of his mouth lifted in something like a smile. Like a smile, but a whole lot more.

Oh, good grief. She knew this type. She'd married one of them and apparently six years of living with a sweet-talking hunk with a roving eye hadn't given her immunity to the breed. 'You don't have to,' she said, quickly. 'Really. I'll be fine.'

'Until you run out of oil.' And he looked up, shading his eyes against the sun. 'If you feel bad about it, you always can make me some more of that shortbread.'

'Oh.' She had known that the shortbread would be misunderstood. 'That was from Clover. For returning her ball. Again.'

'Really?' He didn't sound disappointed. Instead he switched the grin to Clover. 'Nice one, Clover. Tell me, do your talents stretch to making tea?'

Clover giggled. 'Mum made the shortbread. I just put it there to say thank you. But tea's easy.'

'Well, I'm sure your mother could do with a cup. And, since you're making a pot, I like mine with three spoonsful of sugar.'

Clover giggled, again. Stacey fought, with difficulty, the inclination to join in. Clover had an excuse; she was nine years old. At twenty-eight, she knew better. But she was still glad of the excuse to escape to the garage and get her features under proper control while she fetched the toolbox.

'I brought the box,' she said, dropping the toolbox beside him on the grass. They'd inherited it with the house and there was nothing less than fifty years old in it. 'You should find something that fits.'

He folded himself up, opened the box and checked out the contents, testing a couple of spanners against the nuts. 'Okay, we're in business,' he said. Stacey watched, chewing anxiously on her bottom lip, as he began to strip down the mower. Mike used to begin like that. Full of confidence. Nash glanced up, saw her expression. 'Don't look so worried. I'll put it back together again.'

Stacey swallowed. Mike used to say that too. 'I'll, um, get on with trimming the edges of the lawn, then.'

He just smiled and carried on taking her precious, if difficult, mower to bits. She couldn't bear to watch. Instead she worked her way slowly round the edge of the lawn with a pair of long-handled clippers that, too late, she realised were in dire need of sharpening. She just wasn't into the razor-edged lawn look.

She struggled on, hoping Nash wouldn't notice.

It had taken her a while to learn to bite her tongue rather than say, 'I really could do with a shelf...' or 'Have you noticed that cracked tile in the bathroom...' or 'Let's decorate the dining room...'

Mike had thrown himself into everything, but she'd eventually caught on to the fact that his enthusiasm outstripped his competence by a country mile. And that when things went wrong his enthusiasm ran out fast. But he'd been dead for three years and she was out of practice.

She glanced quickly over her shoulder at Nash. If he messed up, she would be in big trouble. She might not keep her lawn short, but she had to keep it manageable so that the girls had somewhere to play. And grass didn't stop growing just because the mower was out of action.

Clover put a mug of tea down beside her, then carried one across to Nash and stayed beside him to watch what he was doing. 'Clover, don't get in the way,' she called out.

'She's fine.' Nash patted the grass beside him, inviting her to sit down, and began to explain what all the bits were and what they did. Rosie, not to be left out, sidled up and joined them. 'This is a washer, and this is a nut,' he began, holding out his hand so that they could check them out. 'And this bolt goes through here, see?' He leaned back so that they could have a good look. 'Then you put the washer on the end of it... Do you want to do that, Rosie?' Rosie giggled. 'You are Rosie, aren't you?'

'Her real name's Primrose,' Clover said. 'But nobody calls her that.'

'I like Primrose,' Rosie protested.

'"'Primrose first-born child of Ver, Merry Springtime's Harbinger...'"' he quoted. 'I bet your birthday's in March.'

'It is,' she said, a little breathless from the attention. 'It is.'

'Okay, Primrose.' He offered her the washer and she took it and put it where he showed her. 'That's right. And now the nut goes on here to hold it all together. Clover, can you do that for me?' Clover carefully screwed it into place. 'Hey, we'll have this done in no time.'

Stacey watched, her heart aching for her girls, for the way it should have been for them. Not that it would have been. Their father had never had that kind of patience.

Nash glanced up, and when he saw she was watching he raised his brows, as if saying, Is this okay? She forced her lips into a smile and then turned away and carried on forcing the blunt shears through the lawn edges.

'Mummy, your tea's getting cold.'

'Oh, sorry.' She stopped, stooped to pick up the mug and, despite herself, turned back to watch. 'Do you have children of your own, Nash?' her mouth enquired, before her brain could stop it.

'No. No children. No wife.' He handed Clover another nut and looked up. 'I'm a rolling stone. I've never stopped travelling long enough to gather any moss.'

She remembered him saying that he'd stayed in worse places than the garden centre. 'Where?'

'All over.' He must have seen the next question in her eyes, or maybe he just knew what was coming. 'I started with VSO in South-East Asia... That's Voluntary Services Overseas,' he explained.

'I've heard of it.' Had thought, once, that she would do that after college. Before she'd met Mike and anything but being with him had suddenly seemed pointless.

'I did a couple of years with them before working on a project with Oxfam. Then I moved on to South America. I've been there for about five years.'

'And now you're home.'

He thought about that for a moment. 'Yes, I suppose I am.' He sounded surprised. As if he couldn't quite believe it. 'Hey, girls, I think this is about done. Let's give it a whirl, shall we?'

He dropped the tools back into the box and gave the mower a push. The blades whirled smoothly, without the grinding noise she'd assumed was due to age and neglect and just something that had to be lived with. 'It sounds so different,' Stacey said. 'What did you do?'

'Nothing much. There was some stuff wrapped around one of the gears. Now I've cleared it, you shouldn't have any more trouble.' He glanced at the shears. 'I could sharpen those for you, if you like. There's a grindstone over there.' He nodded in the direction of the wall and his hair flopped over his forehead. He pushed it back and left a streak of oil on his forehead. It was all she could do to stop herself from reaching up to wipe it away…

'Um…'

'If you like?'

She had the uncomfortable feeling that her mouth had been open. 'I don't want to put you to any bother.'

'It's no bother.' He grinned. 'Honest. I'll do it now, while you're finishing off the grass.'

She'd been afraid he was going to offer to do that, too. Not that she was averse to help. Just unused to it being offered by anyone capable of taking things into their own hands.

Her parents had elected for a grandchild-free retirement in the sun, and although her sister nagged and offered money when she couldn't be side-tracked, Dee was too busy with her high-flying career and her social life to ever just turn up in working clothes with a clean paintbrush ready to help.

Doing everything by yourself was so damned lonely. Maybe Dee was right. She did need a man about the house.

Nash moved the toolbox to the path, not taking it back to the garage, not crowding her as he picked up the shears. 'It'll only take a few minutes. Thanks for the tea, Clover.' And he tossed the shears over the wall and then pulled himself up and over in one fluid movement and dropped down to the other side. The garden seemed very empty without him.

'Can Nash stay to supper, Mummy?' Rosie asked.

'I expect he's busy,' Stacey said. Certainly too

busy to spend the evening with a woman who wasn't as diligent as she should be with the handcream and who needed lavish amounts of moisturiser to keep her complexion looking dewy. Looking like that, he was sure to have every available woman in the neighbourhood fluttering well-mascara'd lashes in his direction. And some of the unavailable ones, too, probably.

'But you'll ask him, won't you?' Clover asked.

The temptation was there; she was only human after all. But she'd learned a little common sense over the years. Enough not to fall twice for a good-looking hunk in a pair of cut-offs. She could be sensible. She might not like it, but she had enough problems without that.

'We'll see,' she said. And applied the mower vigorously to the lawn in order to put an end of the conversation. Even so, she'd only just finished when he reappeared at the top of the wall.

'Nash, Mummy says you can stay to supper if you like,' Clover blurted out, before she could stop her.

'Please say yes,' Rosie pleaded.

Nash took one look at Stacey's face and knew that Clover had put her mother on the spot. He'd planned simply to return the shears, hand them over and retreat. He didn't want to crowd her. She was a widow with two little girls and she was right to be wary of a stranger who'd pitched his tent on the other side of her garden wall.

'Did she?' he asked. Leaving her with no choice but to confirm her daughter's invitation. He wasn't proud of himself but, well, he had to take whatever chances came his way. He didn't plan to be around for long.

'It's nothing exciting,' she said, quickly. 'Spaghetti bolognese.' Then, perhaps realising that she had sounded less than welcoming, she added, 'It's the girls' favourite.'

'Mine, too. But I don't want to make a nuisance of myself. I only looked in to say thanks for the shortbread.' Oh, that was bad. Now she would be forced to repeat the invitation.

'And stayed to fix the mower. It's like a new machine.'

He shrugged. 'It's nothing. When you're two days' drive from the nearest town, you soon learn how to fix things yourself.'

Oh, was that how it was done? 'Well, I'm very grateful. Really. And you're most welcome to eat with us.' She was, Stacey told herself, only being neighbourly. If he'd moved in next door she wouldn't have thought twice. Maybe it was time she did. Think before she opened her mouth. Of course, her sister would disapprove… That thought was sufficient to bring a smile to her lips. 'If you'd like to?'

'The truth? I'd love to. I haven't eaten a home-cooked meal in months.' Which put her in her place. 'What time?'

'About six?'

'I won't be late.' He handed down the shears. Sharpened, re-set and gleaming with oil. Her sister was definitely right. A capable man about the house might not be such a bad idea after all. Just so long as he was the capable man of her choice.

* * *

Stacey looked at her hands, groaned and reached for the nailbrush, promising herself that she would be good and wear gloves in the garden. And she would start using the expensive handcream. *Really*. Just the minute she could find it.

Then she caught sight of herself in the mirror and quickly pulled off the band holding her hair away from her face. And groaned again. Why couldn't she have picked up one of Rosie's pretty bobbles? The one with the little bunch of daisies? Or the butterflies? What on earth had she been thinking of when she had tied her hair back with a plastic cartoon figure of a duck in a sailor suit?

Not much, clearly. She certainly hadn't been thinking of herself as a 'woman'. Well, she hadn't thought of herself in that way for some time. She was a mother. And the crazy woman who grew weeds in her garden and actually put them into pots and expected people to buy them. She made a mean compost heap, though, and had a vegetable garden to die for...

She was just out of the habit of thinking of herself as a woman.

As she scrubbed the green grass stains from her fingers, she sternly told herself that she would have to try harder. Forget Nash Gallagher; at this rate, Lawrence Fordham would take one look and retreat to the bar on Saturday night, black dress notwithstanding.

Lord, but she was a mess. She rinsed off her hands and ran her fingers through her hair, shaking it loose. She'd washed it that morning, but hadn't bothered with a conditioner. She leaned closer to the glass. It showed. Well, it was too late now, and she swept it back in a velvet scrunch. Not exactly sophistication, but anything was an improvement on the duck.

And what on earth was she going to wear?

Then she straightened and looked her reflection right in the eye. 'Who do you think you're kidding, Stacey O'Neill?' she demanded. 'It doesn't matter that your nails haven't seen polish in months. It doesn't matter that your hair hasn't been conditioned to extra gloss. Nash Gallagher isn't going to notice.'

And she'd die of embarrassment if he thought she'd been making a special effort. The last thing she wanted was for him to think she was making eyes at him. He'd probably be more embarrassed than she was.

He was just a kind man who'd fixed her lawnmower in return for some home-baked cookies and then been cornered by Clover and Rosie into staying for supper. At least they'd be eating early and he could escape in time to get on with his life.

Jeans. That was it. She'd wear her good jeans. Good, not as in 'sexy designer jeans', but good as in still in one piece. Okay, so they'd do her the favour of hiding her gardener's knees, but that was the total extent of her vanity. Actually it wasn't vanity, it was a kindness. Her knees would almost certainly put him off his spaghetti.

Her jeans and a white baggy T-shirt, then. Just right.

Except that her legs were hot and tingly from their

sudden exposure to sunlight and the jeans itched, uncomfortably.

Okay. No problem. She had a skirt somewhere. A cream dirndl thing, old, but tidy. It didn't look quite right with the T-shirt, though.

She had that dark red tank-top, one of Dee's cast-offs. Not bad. And perhaps just a touch of mascara. She wouldn't want him to think she wasn't making an effort. It wouldn't be polite. But absolutely no lipstick. None. She regarded her reflection.

Well, maybe just a little gloss.

As she smoothed it across her mouth, she noticed the slight flush, like a quick pass with the blusher, heightening the colour of her cheekbones.

It exactly matched the tension in the pit of her stomach, that tingle of excitement, the urgent need to swallow...

'Clover, Rosie!' she called, as she reached the kitchen. They appeared with suspicious speed, looking desperately eager to help. They knew she had every right to be cross with them. But she wasn't. She was only cross with herself. 'Will you set the table, please?' she said.

'We've done it.' Oh, Lord, so they had. And they'd gone to town with her best cutlery and china. Even used her linen napkins. Well, maybe it didn't matter. Maybe he'd think they always ate like this. 'Can we pick some flowers?' Rosie asked. Flowers? He would really think she was on the make if there were flowers on the table. 'Pleeese,' she begged.

Clover joined in. 'Can we pick some dog roses?'

'*Rosa canina,*' she corrected, automatically.

Definitely not. Absolutely, definitely not. 'You'll scratch yourself on the thorns and the petals will fall off before you get them inside. Just pick something bright and cheerful. You can use that terracotta jug.' It would look suitably childish.

They raced off while she tied an apron around her waist and filled a pan with water for the spaghetti. The sauce was already made and she took it from the fridge, hoping that it would stretch. They'd better have the tart she'd made for lunch tomorrow. She fetched a pint of milk from the fridge and started to make some custard.

The hall clock began to chime. Oh, heck! It was later than she'd thought…all that faffing about with clothes and make-up. Now she'd have to talk to him until the food was ready. What did grown-ups talk about these days?

If only she'd had a drink of some kind to offer him. Something other than the bottle of sticky ginger liqueur she'd won on the tombola at the village fête. The only alternative was blackcurrant juice. The sugar-free stuff that was kind to the teeth. Then her scalp prickled warningly and she glanced up.

Nash was already in the garden. Wearing jeans and a dark blue shirt, his hair glinting creamy gold in the sun. It was like being seventeen again, with Mike waiting for her at the gate with his motorcycle and her mother with a face that would curdle milk…

'Careful,' she cautioned, on automatic, as Rosie filled the terracotta jug at the sink. But she continued to stir the custard, not taking her eyes off Nash as he walked through her garden, stopping to take in her bold planting of Rosebay Willow Herb and Queen Anne's Lace.

Then he turned, caught her watching him with a stupid grin plastered all over her face and he smiled right back, leaving her in no doubt that he'd been very kind to his teeth all his life.

Behind her there was a scream and a crash.

CHAPTER FOUR

NASH paused in the open doorway and with one swift look took in the disaster. Broken jug, flowers, water everywhere and Rosie close to tears. 'Am I too early?'

Stacey should have—normally would have—recognised the potential disaster in allowing a seven-year-old to put flowers on the table and kept a close eye on her. Not that she could have anticipated a spider dropping onto Rosie's hand as she carried the jug across the kitchen.

'I can take a walk around the garden and pretend I didn't see this, if you like.'

Stacey, carefully picking pieces of pottery out of the spreading puddle of water, looked up. She shouldn't have worried about trying to impress him. Children would bring you down to earth every time. 'No, come on in. If you can find somewhere safe to walk.'

'In that case, can I do anything to help?' Her surprise must have shown because he added, 'I can handle a mop.'

'Can you?' He looked like every woman's private fantasy and he was domesticated, too? Stacey, momentarily tempted to put this extraordinary statement to the test, forced her fluttering hormones back into the cage marked 'Danger—Do Not Feed'. 'No,

I'm fine.' She stood up, dumped the pieces of broken jug in the bin and reached for a mop, while he helped Clover pick the flowers out of the puddle. 'Well, very nearly fine. I've just realised I can't offer you a drink, unless you happen to enjoy blackcurrant cordial? South side of the supermarket,' she added, wondering if she sounded as hysterical as she felt. 'A precocious little vintage, absolutely packed with vitamin C...'

'I'm seriously tempted,' he said. 'But I found that languishing in my cellar and I thought you might like to help me drink it before the sell-by date runs out.' He nodded in the direction of a bottle of red wine he'd put on the table.

Wine. That was so...grown up. She'd been living in a children's world for so long, she'd forgotten what that was like.

Wine. Oh, crikey. Stacey tried not to panic. She had a corkscrew. She just couldn't remember the last time she'd seen it. Or where. 'Your tent has a cellar?' she asked, giving herself a moment or two to think.

'Hasn't everyone's?' Nash produced a chunky penknife from his back pocket, opened it up to reveal a corkscrew and set to work on the bottle.

Clearly he was a man who came prepared for any eventuality, she thought. And the hormones threw themselves against the bars, howling to be let out.

'We've got a cellar,' Rosie said, distracting her. 'There's nothing in it, though, except for spiders.' And she shuddered from the safety of the doorway. 'It was a spider on the flowers that caused the accident,' Stacey explained, quickly. 'Rosie doesn't like them.'

'There's nothing wrong with spiders, Primrose. They do all kinds of good stuff.' She didn't look convinced. 'They eat flies for a start. And mosquitoes. When I was in the jungle…' He produced a couple of cans of cola from his pockets and glanced at Stacey. 'Are these allowed?'

How like a man to ask when it was already impossible to say no. It was niggling to complain, she knew. She should be grateful for any evidence that he wasn't absolutely perfect. Something her head could have told her, any time. Perfect did not happen. Unfortunately, her body had never quite cottoned on to that fact.

'Just this once,' she warned. For the girls' benefit. She didn't anticipate this happening again.

Before she could add, on automatic, Not-out-of-the-can, Clover ripped the ring pull, swallowed a mouthful, wiped her mouth on the back of her hand and asked, 'Were you really in the jungle, Nash?'

'I certainly was. And when I was in the jungle,' he continued, 'a spider saved my life.'

'How?' Rosie's voice was little more than a whisper. It was like poking a sore tooth, Stacey thought. Horrible, but irresistible.

Nash pulled the cork from the bottle and set it on the table. 'Are you sure you can handle this? It was a really big spider—'

'How big?' Clover demanded.

Responding to the eagerness in her voice, he made a circle with his hands. 'Big as a dinner plate.'

He couldn't know that Clover was just winding up her little sister, but as Rosie visibly shuddered, he quickly caught on. 'Well, maybe, more like a tea plate,' he said, quickly downsizing the scare. 'His name was Roger—'

Gorgeous, domesticated, far-sighted and quick on his feet... How could anyone be scared of a spider called Roger? 'How do you know he was called Roger?' Stacey asked, encouraging him to keep it cute. 'Did he tell you?'

Nash looked affronted. 'Certainly not. Spiders are very private creatures and there's an etiquette about these things. A parrot introduced us.' Clover giggled. So, remarkably, did Rosie. 'He had a particular weakness for cheese sandwiches...'

'Who? Roger?'

'No.' He glanced at her and for a moment it was as if they were alone on the planet. She knew this. She'd done this before. If they'd been alone, the food would have burned to a cinder unnoticed... 'The parrot.'

'Oh.' She was floundering. Dry-mouthed and floundering. She'd forgotten how it could be, forgotten that recognition...

'I like parrots,' Rosie said, easing away from the door.

Stacey turned away, stuffed the flowers in a small china jug and set it in the middle of the table, then reached down a couple of glasses from the dresser. Her hands were steady, she noticed. How could that be when the rest of her was shaking like an aspen? Nash poured out the wine and handed a glass to her.

His hands were steady, too. Rock steady. How were his insides doing?

She swallowed. She didn't want to know. She really didn't want to know.

'Could we have a parrot?' Clover asked.

'No, we couldn't,' Stacey said, just a bit too sharply. Then, 'Maybe a budgie, or a cockatiel when we move.' If she said it out loud often enough, she might get used to the idea.

'You're moving?' Nash asked.

'No!' Rosie glared at her. 'We're not. We're going to stay here for ever and ever!'

Stacey swallowed. She had been thinking about herself, hating the thought of moving into something small, in town, leaving her garden, her little greenhouse, her lovely rickety potting shed… This was a problem she hadn't anticipated. Not that she went looking for them. She already had more problems than she knew what to do with.

She certainly didn't need Nash Gallagher stirring up a hornets' nest in her hormones.

'Have you got any pets, Primrose?' Nash asked, cutting through the sudden tension.

Clover giggled and Rosie glared at her. 'No. Daddy wanted a dog, but he was allergic to them,' she said. 'Do you think he's got a dog now he's in heaven?'

Nash had been feeling his way with the girls. Teasing them a little. Catching the look of panic that had crossed Stacey's face when Rosie shuddered. Most children enjoyed being scared, but she was a child who needed a lot of reassurance, he guessed.

Losing her daddy must have been hard to understand.

Clover was tougher. 'I don't see why not,' he said, matter-of-factly. 'I shouldn't think anyone suffers from allergies in heaven.'

He glanced at Stacey but she turned away quickly before he could catch her expression. Did she still pine for her dead husband? She put down the glass and made a performance of checking to see if the spaghetti was cooked. How long had it been since he'd died? he wondered.

'One more minute,' Stacey said, briskly. 'Sit down, everyone, while I dish up.'

'Is there anything I can do?' he asked.

'No, thanks.' Then she half turned. Half smiled. 'I'm not used to domesticated men.'

'In my case it's necessity. Maybe I can help wash up?'

'You can come again.' And then she blushed. Not much, just a faint betraying heat to colour her cheekbones, a heat that found an echoing response in his own blood.

The sensible thing to do would be to put some distance between them, and fast. She was a young widow with children and that was far too complicated for a man who liked to travel light and keep moving.

But there was something about Stacey. From the moment she'd climbed that wall he hadn't been able to get her out of his head.

Stacey couldn't believe she'd said that. That was almost…flirting! Definitely time to get a grip. 'I'm sorry we're having to eat in the kitchen,' she said, formally, 'but the dining room is being redecorated.'

Clover looked up at her in surprise. About to say that they always ate in the kitchen, she caught Stacey's warning look and changed her mind. 'Have you got a dog, Nash?' she asked, instead.

'I'm never in one place long enough to keep animals,' he said. 'I had one when I was your age, though.'

'What kind?'

'A bit of this and a bit of that,' he said. 'Quite a lot of dalmatian.'

Rosie sighed. 'I love dalmatians,' she said.

'She loves the film about them,' Stacey corrected.

'Can we watch it after tea? You'd like to see it, Nash, wouldn't you?'

'I'm sure Nash has far more exciting things to do than watch a film with you, Rosie.'

'Nothing that won't keep,' he said. So much for keeping his distance. Then he grinned. 'I won't mind if you want to get on with your paper-hanging.'

'Paper-hanging?'

'In the dining room.'

There was no doubt about it, Stacey decided, Nash Gallagher was a teaser. He teased the children and now he was teasing her. Just how old did he think she was? That kind of thing was fine when you were a kid, when you were young and silly and didn't have to worry about where the money was coming from to pay the electric bill.

It was fine if you were just looking for some fun with no strings attached. There probably wasn't much to choose between them for age, but while she was having to be sensible, Nash was just passing through.

And he was in his prime while she...well, women aged faster than men.

Of course, she did have other attractions. In fact, if you overlooked the gardener's hands and the fact that her perky bits didn't perk quite as snappily as they had before she'd had her babies, she still had quite a bit going for her.

She was handy for work, unattached and, thanks to Clover, he had ample evidence that she wasn't a bad cook.

Maybe that was why he was so determined to convince her that he was domesticated. Maybe he could see the advantages. A well-laid table to get his feet under and a soft billet with a merryish widow would, no doubt, fit the bill nicely until he moved on.

Heck, he probably thought she'd be grateful for the attention.

Dee was right. She should be looking for more from a man than a body like a Greek statue and a smile to melt ice. She'd make a real effort to be nice to Lawrence on Saturday, she promised herself.

'Parmesan?' she said, discouragingly, offering him the cheese that Dee had brought her back from her spring holiday in Italy, along with the grater so that he could help himself.

Nash knew he'd pushed his luck a touch too far. He'd pushed and for a moment she'd been enjoying herself. Then the guilt had got to her. Widowed mothers weren't supposed to have fun.

He knew it the moment she banged the cheese dish down beside him.

'This is good,' he said, after a few moments of uncomfortable silence when even the children seemed to recognise the need to keep their heads down and concentrate on their food.

'Thank you. Clover, will you please pour that drink into a glass?' She turned back to him. 'So, Nash, what did you do in South America?'

The whole tone had changed, he realised. The way she was holding herself, the brisk politeness in her voice. She'd stopped being sweet and soft and a little bit out of her depth and was suddenly behaving like a dowager at a garden party. The vulnerability that he had glimpsed, that he had felt himself responding to in the way a flower responds to the sun, had been firmly suppressed. Now she was just being professionally polite.

She was *that* vulnerable? But he took his tone from her. 'I was looking for plants.'

'Looking for plants?' A spark of interest. Well, she was obviously enthusiastic about her native flora.

'I'm a botanist. The rainforest is full of plants that no one has ever seen before. I was on a collecting trip.'

'For five years?'

'It's a big place.' He could see that she was struggling to equate the idea of him as a botanist with the man who was apparently labouring next door.

He picked up the wine bottle and topped up her glass. 'Botany doesn't pay very well,' he offered.

She raised a sceptical eyebrow. 'Obviously not, if you have to moonlight as a labourer.'

So she thought he was stretching the truth—well that wasn't a problem. But he didn't want her to be too sure. 'It's worse than that. No one will employ you until you've had field experience. And you can't get field experience until someone will employ you. That's why I did the voluntary work overseas.'

'Even so...' She hesitated. 'Surely you could do better than a labouring job?'

'Probably. In fact, my father takes the view that I should stop messing about and get a proper job.'

'Oh? What does he have in mind?'

'A career in a bank, or insurance, or even working for a supermarket chain.'

'Oh, *seriously* sensible stuff.' And she laughed. She understood why that was impossible, he thought. But then he'd always known she would.

'I think you could describe my father as a sensible man,' he agreed. He'd married for money instead of love. That was seriously sensible. 'He thinks I should be paying more attention to the future. To my pension plan.'

'I've got a sister like that. Maybe they've got a point.'

'Maybe, but I like to be out in the open.'

'Since you're sleeping in a tent, that's probably just as well.'

'Yes, well, the tent is the only accommodation

around here. Unless you know anyone in the village who'd take pity on a homeless botanist?'

'I'm afraid not,' Stacey said quickly, before Clover could offer him the spare room. She'd call in at the village shop first thing on Monday morning and take her card down before he saw it. She wanted a student. She could handle a student. There was no way she could handle running into Nash on the landing in his boxer shorts. 'If I hear of something I'll let you know.'

'Thanks.' She sipped her wine, toyed with her spaghetti, looked a little flushed. Did she think he was angling for a bed in the spare room? Nash wondered. Or maybe even offering to fill the empty half of her own double bed. Well, maybe she was right. The idea of cosying up to Stacey in a big soft bed was giving his body the kind of ideas that had no place at a family table. 'What about you, Stacey?' he said, in an effort to distract himself. 'Do you have a job?'

'I do some gardening.'

'Oh? I can see you're an enthusiast; I didn't realise you were a professional.'

'Hardly that.' She shrugged. 'I started a course in horticulture at the local college but life got in the way before I finished it.'

Marriage and motherhood. Or maybe it was the other way around. 'You should go back and finish the course. You'd get a grant, wouldn't you?'

'Maybe. But... Well, you can't go back. And I put what I learned to good use. I've started selling some of the plants I grow but I need a proper outlet.

The cowslips and violets are very popular at the village shop, but well—' they scarcely covered the water rates '—it's a bit limited.'

Stacey stopped. She was moving into a neat, easy to manage little house in town. She'd get a job in an office and stop dreaming.

'Wild flowers?' Nash prompted.

'A dream of mine.' A stupid dream. She snapped on a smile. 'Maybe you'll find a protected species of wild flower next door and then they won't be able to develop the site,' she said.

There was a slight pause, and then he said, 'I'll be sure to keep an eye out for one.'

She glanced up, suspicious of his gravity. He wasn't smiling. At least, not that she could tell. 'How's it going over there? Any news when work will start?'

'Not yet.'

Oh, God, this was fun. Rosie and Clover were subdued, she was embarrassed, Nash was...well, Nash was undoubtedly regretting his kind impulse in leaving the strawberries. In fixing the mower.

Stacey silently groaned. She was a cow. Nash Gallagher had been nothing but kind and here she was, implying the worst of motives to his actions. She emptied her glass and forced a smile.

'Eat up,' she said, brightly. 'It's gooseberry tart and custard for pudding.'

Nash pushed back his chair and got to his feet. 'That was great, Stacey. A real treat.'

'You're welcome.'

'Come on, Clover, Primrose. Let's clear this table and make your mother a cup of coffee.'

'There's no need, really.'

'I don't agree. In fact I think you should go and put your feet up while we wash up.'

'Oh, but...'

He tutted warningly. 'Trust me. I'm a doctor.'

'A doctor?'

'Well, I've got a PhD.'

And he was labouring? Oh, yes, sure. Pull the other one, why don't you, and see how loud it rings? She wasn't sure whether she was flattered that he felt he had to impress her, or cross that he would lie to do it. 'Does a philosophy doctorate count?' she asked, without bothering to hide her disbelief.

He just grinned, apparently not the least bit offended. 'It'll cover doing the dishes. Go and set up the video and we'll be right with you.'

To protest further would be petulant. By the time she'd found the film and loaded it into the video Nash appeared, carrying a tray set with her prettiest mugs and a cafetière of fresh coffee.

She crossed to the sofa, expecting the girls to come and cuddle up next to her, the way they usually did. Nash beat them to it. He put the tray on the low table by the sofa and sat down beside her. It was a long time since she'd shared a sofa with a man. This one, old and saggy, propelled them against one another. He smelled of fresh air. Like clean washing.

She unpeeled her tongue from the roof of her

mouth. 'Wouldn't you be more comfortable in the armchair, Nash?'

He glanced at it, then looked back down into her face. 'I can see much better from here,' he said.

Rosie and Clover didn't help, happily dragging their floor cushions over to the sofa and curling up at their feet to watch the film.

This was how it would have been if Mike was alive, she thought. The four of them. Maybe. Her gaze strayed from the screen to the man sitting beside her, with his thick, pale hair, his body to die for. He leaned forward to pour the coffee, brushing against her arm.

'Milk?' he asked, turning to her. 'Sugar?' His smile would melt ice.

'Just milk,' she said. He handed her a mug. 'Thank you.'

'You're welcome.' He sat back, totally at home, his coffee in one hand, his other arm stretched out along the back of the sofa. Not quite touching her shoulders.

She tried to imagine Lawrence Fordham sitting there in his place, watching a Disney film with Rosie and Clover, laughing out loud at the funny bits, suitably outraged at the antics of the villainous Cruella de Ville...

Her imagination refused to make the leap.

CHAPTER FIVE

'ALL right, girls. That's it. Bedtime.' There were the usual pleas that it was Saturday and they didn't have school, but Stacey was firm. 'Now, please. Say goodnight to Nash. You've got five minutes before I come up to tuck you in.'

''Night, Nash.' Rosie flung her arms about his neck and gave him a hug. He stood up with her, carried her to the stairs and placed her on the bottom step before ruffling her curls.

'Goodnight, sweetheart.'

Clover, older, was more reserved about showing her feelings. 'Will you come again tomorrow, Nash? We could play football.'

'Clover!' The child's invitation was as bright as her smile, but behind it Stacey saw a raw need. Her little girls wanted a daddy. 'I'm sure Nash has more important things to do than play football.'

But Clover was treated to the kind of smile that would knock the socks off any girl. Or her mother. Her little girls wanted a daddy...which was not the same thing at all as her wanting a man.

'There's nothing I'd rather do, sweetheart,' he said, 'but I have to visit someone tomorrow.'

Clover looked crestfallen. 'Monday, then?'

'Clover,' Stacey warned again. 'Don't be pushy. And don't forget your teeth.' The girls retreated reluctantly up the stairs, leaving her alone with Nash. 'I'm sorry,' she began. 'Please don't—'

'I won't,' he said, before she could finish. He wouldn't what? His voice was reassuring. His expression less easy to read. He wouldn't allow Clover to manipulate him? Or was he promising her that he wouldn't make a nuisance of himself? The easy smile had faded to something that might just hint at self-mockery. 'I'll leave you to put the girls to bed. Thank you, Stacey. It's been a lovely evening.'

Her heart said, It needn't be over. Stay. I'll put the girls to bed, make some fresh coffee and maybe we could even try a glass of that liqueur...

Her mouth said, 'You're easy to please.'

'You think so?'

There was a moment, a pause when anything might have happened, and Stacey found herself harbouring the briefest longing to be kissed by Nash, a longing immediately followed by panic that her wish would be fulfilled.

It had been so long. She wouldn't know what to do, how to react...

'Mummy! There's no toothpaste!'

The moment was swept away in the mundane, but the edge of disappointment was sharp enough for her to be left in no doubt which feeling had been the most powerful.

'Go and see to them, Stacey. I'll make my own way out.'

He hadn't touched her and yet she felt as if his fingers had brushed against her cheek. He hadn't kissed her and yet her mouth was hot and throbbing.

She'd forgotten how it was. What desire did. The way it stole your wits and made a fool of you.

Nash lay back on his sleeping bag, contemplating the star-strewn heaven and wondering what on earth he was doing. He had always made a point of keeping his life simple.

A childhood spent with parents who took pleasure from making one another unhappy had given him an aversion to complications and he'd reached the age of thirty-three without encountering any convincing reason to change his mind.

He'd been passing through, that was all. Spending a day or two with his grandfather, making his peace with the old man before he left. From what he'd seen, it was clear that if he agreed to lead the collecting trip to Central America, they wouldn't meet again.

But his grandfather wasn't done with life just yet. He might be frail, but he still enjoyed pulling strings, manipulating people. And Nash had indulged him. Let him believe he was getting away with it. It was little enough to do for an old man...

'Just call in, Nash. Someone should. To say goodbye. I didn't have the chance. Well, I was carried out of there on a stretcher.' The old reprobate knew how to tug the heart strings, Nash thought, grinning despite himself. Then his grandfather had added the clincher. 'I'd go myself, but they won't let me out of here.' He'd have offered to smuggle him out, but he thought it might be better if the old man didn't see the way his garden had deteriorated without constant loving care and attention. 'Come back on Sunday and tell me how it is. I'll sign the papers then.'

Nothing was ever that simple, Nash thought. Certainly not his grandfather. Not that he had been fooled. He could read the subtext as clearly as if it had been written on the nursing home wall.

When you've been back, visited the past, I'll sign the papers and consign centuries of devoted husbandry to the developer's skip, if that's what you want. But I'm not letting you off that easily. You've got to look the past in the eye before you make the decision.

He'd known what to expect, but it had still come as a shock to see such dereliction. How long he would have remained there, wallowing in nostalgia for the past, if Stacey O'Neill hadn't climbed over the wall, if he hadn't found himself drowning in a pair of eyes the colour of clear honey, was now academic.

The peach trees might have touched an unexpected vein of sentiment, a longing for a simpler time in a place where he'd been happy, but Stacey's eyes, her blushing smile, had tantalised him with the idea that he might be happy again.

But it was complicated. Seriously complicated. She wasn't just some girl he could love and then move on if he discovered that he was chasing a will-o'-the-wisp fantasy. She was a woman with young children. They came as a package and the one thing he'd learned, knew above all others, was that children should never be hurt by the carelessness of those old enough to know better.

So the simple thing, the common sense thing, would be to walk away now. From the garden, from Stacey, from Clover and Primrose.

So why did keeping things simple suddenly seem to have lost its appeal? Why was it taking all his will power not to climb back over the wall and get seriously complicated?

Tomorrow. He'd pack up tomorrow. Call at the nursing home, as he'd promised, and then get on with the totally uncomplicated life he'd planned.

The sun had brought out the honeysuckle and it smelt like heaven. Stacey stood at the back door, reluctant to close it against the night and go to bed.

She shook her head. Kidding herself. Her restlessness had nothing to do with the honeysuckle climbing into the old apple tree at the end of the garden. It was the man beyond the wall that had her standing in the darkness of the garden like some silly girl hoping for a knight in shining armour to leap it, promising her all manner of excitement.

She'd been there, done that. Well, maybe not *quite* that. But Mike's motorcycle had come pretty close. Exciting enough, anyway, for a seventeen-year-old with a romantic streak a mile wide.

But she wasn't seventeen any more. It was time to face reality. Nash Gallagher would be moving on in a week or two. Dating Lawrence Fordham was about as exciting as her life was going to get from here on in.

She shut the door and locked it and went to bed, determined to forget all about Nash with his cornsilk hair and his heart-stealing smile.

But the scent of honeysuckle seeped in through her open window and mocked her.

For a man who could sleep on the proverbial clothes-line, Nash was having a bad night. After a while he gave up trying, rolled onto his back and, linking his hands beneath his head, thought about the past, thought about the garden. All his best memories had been made here.

Some things never changed.

Stacey tossed and turned until her nightie had become so twisted that she was compelled to get out of bed and shake it loose. The night was so short that the trees were already clearly visible against the sky and there seemed little point in staying in bed. She felt like doing something energetic and noisy to chase away the half-dreams that had disturbed her.

She glanced at the clock. It was only just past four o'clock on a Sunday morning. Far too early to be noisy.

Maybe if she made some tea, took a walk around the garden to clear her head, she could get back to sleep.

She opened the window a little wider for more air and leaned out across the sill. There was the faint glow of a light beyond the wall, a light filtered greenly through canvas. It made her feel a little less lonely to know that she wasn't the only soul awake.

What was he doing? Reading, perhaps. Or writing up his notes. Or maybe he was planning his next research trip.

Research trip? Botanist? She shook her head at her own gullibility. The man was labouring over there. Clearing away the rubbish. Would she never learn?

Apparently not. She pulled on a pair of jogging pants and a T-shirt and went downstairs, put the kettle on. When it boiled, she made a pot of tea and carried the tray outside.

'Nash?' Her whisper sounded like thunder in the pre-dawn silence. A bird chuntered irritably in the apple tree. Her heart beat louder than the whisper.

Nothing. No answer. He'd probably just fallen asleep with his torch still on. Which, considering the way her heart was pounding, was probably just as well. This had to be the stupidest thing on earth... 'Nash?'

'Stacey, is something wrong?'

Oh, Lord. She hadn't heard him coming but his voice, low and urgent, was just the other side of the wall. *This* was heart-pounding... 'No. I saw your light. I've made some tea and I thought you might like some. Stick your head over and I'll pass the mug up to you.'

Nash stood knee-deep in daisies in the darkness. Did she want to keep the wall between them? Or was it an invitation?

He thought he knew, but wasn't sure that she did. He hauled himself up and looked down into her face. Innocent, sweet. Uncertain. Well, that made two of them. But he'd rather be uncertain on the same side of the wall. 'Hold on, I'll come over. It'll be easier.' She didn't object and he jumped down, saw her wince as he flattened some favourite plant. 'Maybe I should put a gate in there,' he said.

There was an infinitesimal pause before she said, 'It's hardly worth it, when you'll be moving on.'

It was a question, but he didn't have the answer so he countered with one of his own. 'Couldn't you sleep?' he asked.

'No.' His hair was dishevelled, his silvered shoulders and chest naked in the light of the waning moon. 'It's the sudden heat,' she said, suddenly feeling very hot indeed. 'I'd have thought you'd be used to it, though.'

He was. It took a lot more than a warm night to keep him awake, but Stacey O'Neill was managing to do it. The way she'd been looking at him before Clover had claimed her attention was not only keeping him awake but giving him all kinds of disturbing thoughts.

But how did you make love to a woman with two small children under her feet?

The answer appeared to be, when she came looking for you before dawn. Maybe. But not if you were planning on catching a plane to some distant rainforest in the very near future.

'Some things you never get used to,' he said, and took the mug she'd brought him. 'Shall we go and sit on the bench by the back door? In case the girls wake up.' He invoked their sleeping chaperons. Two little gooseberries to keep them on the right side of sanity. He took a sip of tea and then firmly led the way up to the house, away from the temptation of the soft grass beneath his bare feet. At the sound of her voice he hadn't even stopped to put on his boots. 'Your garden smells like heaven at night.'

'Mmmm. It's the honeysuckle.'

'Tell me about your plan to sell wild flowers,' he said.

She glanced at him, as if surprised he remembered. 'I don't have a plan. Just a dream.'

'Have you got space for a commercial enterprise?'

'Probably not. It would help if I stopped growing enough vegetables to keep the entire village in freebies and put up some more greenhouses.'

'I'm sure the village shop would appreciate that.'

'Yeah.' Stacey stared into her mug. But greenhouses required cash. She and Archie had talked about it, and he'd been going to advise her, but then she'd found him slumped over his desk with a stroke.

She really would have to find the time to go and see him again, soon. The nursing home was just too far to cycle, though. Maybe she could persuade Dee to take her. Or even lend her the car for a few hours. After all, Dee owed her a favour.

'Stacey?'

She shook her head. 'Forget it, Nash. I have.'

'Have you?' She wasn't looking at him and he desperately wanted to see her eyes.

Stacey was so aware of him. Aware of herself. It was as if every cell was reaching out for him, urging her to do something stupid. Say something stupid. Like, I don't want to talk about lost dreams. I want to make some new ones.

She was holding onto the feeling so tightly, keeping herself under such a tight rein that she physically jumped when he touched her. 'I don't think so.' Think…think…say something now to stop this. But his fingers grazed her cheek, searing her skin. And she turned, unable to help herself, to confront eyes that were utterly dark, utterly unreadable in the pre-dawn light. 'I don't think so,' he repeated.

'Maybe not,' she admitted, quickly and turned away. 'But there's no point in crying for the moon.'

'No point in crying for it. Reaching for it is something else. Don't give up on your dreams, Stacey.'

'What are your dreams, Nash?'

His hand dropped and he turned away then. 'I'm not much of a dreamer.'

'No?' She forced a teasing smile to her lips. 'But if you're a botanist—' she allowed the doubt to linger in her voice '—surely you must yearn to discover some incredibly important plant that'll be named after you? That's a kind of immortality.'

'Yeah. Maybe.' Then he smiled politely, put the mug on a tray and stood up. 'I'd better go and get on with my own plans. Thanks for the tea.'

'You're welcome,' she said, staying put and watching him walk away down the garden, haul himself over the garden wall. 'Any time.'

'Mummy? What are you doing?'

'Thinking.'

'What about?'

About tiles and things called 'spacers' and a mysterious substance called 'grout' and what colour paint would give the bathroom a 'come-and-live-here' look. More to the point, would her amateurish efforts with a paintbrush make things better? Or worse.

'Nothing much,' she said, turning to Rosie and seeing the big bunch of flowers that she was holding. Big daisies, bright yellow buttercups, Queen Anne's Lace and honeysuckle. 'Where did you get those?' she asked. As if she didn't know.

'They were on the back doorstep.' Yes, well, she hadn't opened the back door since her pre-dawn adventure. In fact she'd been avoiding the garden, although she wasn't sure why. But she couldn't resist touching the silky petals of the flowers, plucking one of them from the middle of the bunch. *Leucanthemum vulgare*. The ox-eye daisy. She loved daisies, especially the tall ones with the big fuzzy yellow centres. 'I suppose Nash must have left them,' Rosie said.

'I suppose he must have.'

'I think he liked having tea with us,' she said. 'He left a note.' A note? Her heart hadn't heard about the 'being sensible' plan and did an excited little flip-flop. 'What note?'

'It just said, ''Thanks for last night''.' She shrugged. 'Something like that.'

'And where is this note?'

'In the kitchen. On the dresser.'

Stacey resisted the urge to race down the stairs to

read it. You could tell so much about a man from his handwriting… 'Why don't you go and put the flowers in some water, hmm?'

'Okay.'

'And, Rosie… Try not to drop the vase.'

'It's okay, Nash put a PS saying he'd checked them for spiders.' Stacey didn't think her younger daughter's reading was up to that standard. Rosie must have seen her doubtful expression, because she said, 'Clover read it.'

'Oh, right.' Stacey swallowed. She wanted to charge down the garden and stick her head over the wall and say, 'Thank you!' and 'Come to breakfast!' and, well, all sorts of stupid things that she didn't even dare think, let alone say out loud.

So, she turned back to the bathroom, twirling the flower between her fingers. Yellow and white, she thought. Like the daisies. It would be fresh and sunny. Cheerful.

She'd cycle up to the Homecare Centre later, when the girls were at football practice on the green. She checked her watch. Much later. It wasn't eight o'clock yet. It was going to be a long day.

She sorted out some plants that were ready for sale. If she could find somewhere to sell them. The petrol station at the end of the village had said they'd take a few wild flower plants if she was prepared to supply them with boxes of bedding plants, too. It wasn't that she had anything against bedding plants. It was just that she'd rather get a job in an office.

She pricked out what seemed like a thousand cowslip seedlings. And dreamed a little.

Finally the girls left to play football, but just as Stacey was getting out her bike her sister pulled into the drive. She'd brought over the Armani dress, a silk suit, a couple of fine jersey sweaters and a skirt which she laid over the sofa. Then she went back to her car and fetched two pairs of shoes, still in their boxes.

She hadn't chosen a great moment to play Lady Bountiful. Stacey wasn't in the mood to be patronised by her big sister with her hand-me-downs. Even when the hand-me-downs had designer labels.

Designer labels weren't a lot of use when you earned your living as a jobbing gardener and self-employed, self-delusioned nurseryperson. What you needed were good boots and cargo trousers and the kind of jumpers that were best bought at jumble sales.

She eyed the clothes and, with suspicion born out of experience, said, 'What do you want?'

'Stacey!' Dee was all injured innocence. 'I had to bring over the dress and when I was looking through my wardrobe it occurred to me that you might have a use for these.' She made it sound as if it would be a favour to take them off her hands. 'They're a bit last season, if you know what I mean.'

'Are they?' She looked at the shoes. A size larger than her sister usually wore. 'And your feet have shrunk, too, have they?'

Dee went just the tiniest bit pink. 'I bought them when I was expecting Harry,' she said, quickly improvising. 'It seems such a dreadful waste to have them just sitting there.'

'I agree,' Stacey said. Dee relaxed a moment. 'I'm sure if you took them back, you'd get a refund.'

'I bought them ages ago. And I don't know what I've done with the receipts.'

This from the woman who filed her supermarket check-out receipts in date order? 'Maybe you should check your handbag,' Stacey suggested, drily. She'd seen those black evening slippers in the window of Dee's favourite boutique the last time she was in town. She repeated her question. 'What do you want, Dee?'

'Okay,' she said. 'Okay. I admit it. I need a favour. A really big favour.'

'You want me to sleep with Lawrence on Saturday night?'

'Would you?' Dee enquired, hopefully.

'No, Dee, I wouldn't.'

'No, perhaps you're right. You'll need to take it gently.'

'Why?' Lawrence was grown man, for heaven's sake. 'Is he a virgin?' She didn't wait for an answer. She didn't really want to know that much about Lawrence Fordham. 'Oh, come on, you can give me a lift to Homecare and I'll let you help me choose the tiles and paint for the bathroom.'

'The bathroom?'

'You said it needed tiling.'

'But I didn't mean...' Then she changed tack. 'Help me out, and I'll pay someone to do it for you.'

'But I'll never learn that way,' Stacey replied, innocently. 'Besides, the girls are going to help. It'll be fun.'

'Will it? Okay, let's go and buy some paint.' Good grief, did she sound that convincing? Or was Dee simply humouring her?

Humouring her. Once she'd suggested a neat way to use the cheapest white and yellow tiles to good effect, she returned to the subject of the favour she wanted. 'The thing is, there's a reception at the Town Hall tomorrow night.'

'Is there? That's nice. How many boxes of these will I need, do you think?'

Dee took a tiny calculator from her bag. 'I was hoping you'd say that,' she said, as she tapped in some figures. 'Lawrence is on the Twinning Committee and I promised I'd go with him.'

'So? Am I supposed to be jealous?'

Dee ignored this. 'The problem is there's a panic over the European marketing of a new organic yoghurt so I have to fly to Paris first thing. It might take a couple of days—'

'And you're going to have to miss the reception? Oh, that's tough…' Stacey's voice trailed off. She'd been so busy winding her sister up that she'd missed the trap.

'Not for me, but it's hard on Lawrence. I talked him into joining the committee because of the European connections, but if I'm not there I know he'll make some excuse not to go.'

He'd dare to do that? Maybe he wasn't such a wimp after all. 'Whatever would he do without you to hold his hand, darling?'

'Without me, darling, he'd still be running a tin-pot little dairy instead of a company heading for the stratosphere. His products are wonderful, but he has absolutely no head for business. You'll need six boxes of the yellow and five of the white, by the way. And some of those edging thingies.' She did another rapid calculation and took some boxes from the shelf. 'You will stand in for me, won't you?'

Stacey offered Dee the paint colour chart. 'This one is closest to the yellow tiles, I think.' Then, 'If you need a stand-in, why don't I go to Paris so that you can stay and make absolutely sure Lawrence doesn't duck his responsibilities?'

Dee perused the chart through narrowed eyes then shook her head. 'This is going to be too much yellow. Paint the walls white and use the yellow with stencils to break it up.' Stencils? Stacey had enough trouble with plain walls without getting complicated. 'I suppose you could go to Paris,' Dee continued doubtfully, choosing a couple of stencils and adding them to the trolley. 'Just how much do you know about marketing organic yoghurt?' she asked, and waited. When there was no response, she grinned. 'That much, huh?' She added a tin of white paint. 'I take it I can tell Lawrence you'll go with him?'

Stacey put the white paint back on the shelf and replaced it with the yellow. 'I'll do it,' she said, returning the stencils to the rack. 'But I need a favour too.' Her sister's eyes narrowed cautiously, but what the heck? She could only say no. 'Since you're not going to be using it on Monday, can I borrow your car?'

Dee blanched. 'You won't put your tools in the boot, will you? Or get mud on the carpets?'

'Well, I wanted to use it to transport a couple of sacks of well-rotted horse manure... No, of course I won't get mud on the carpets! I just want to visit Archie Baldwin. The old man who used to run the garden centre. He's in a nursing home on the other side of Maybridge. It's too far to bike and it'll take all day by public transport.'

'Will he know about the development?'

'I'm just going to visit him, Dee. He's a friend.'

Dee shrugged. 'Okay. I'll need it this evening, but I'll drop it off on my way to the airport. I'll be leaving at some unearthly hour, so I'll shove the keys through the letterbox.'

'Thanks.'

'No problem. You'll be able to drive yourself to the hairdresser.' Stacey opened her mouth to protest. 'On expenses. This is business. Wear the silk two-piece and the shoes with the kitten heels.'

Protest was clearly pointless. 'Yes, miss. Whatever you say, miss.'

'Perfect answer, darling. For that, you get the voile tied-blind on me.'

'What voile tied-blind?'

'That one. You'll need *something* to break up all that yellow.' As Dee tossed it into the trolley, Stacey resisted with the greatest difficulty an urge to lie down on the floor, drum her heels and scream.

CHAPTER SIX

'So, how bad is it?'

Nash stared out of the window at the manicured lawns of the nursing home. 'Do you want me to tell you, Archie? Really?' He turned to face the frail old man sitting in the wheelchair. 'You must know what neglect does to a garden.'

'I know. I just wasn't sure that you did. And not just to a garden. People need a little tender loving care, too.' Then, 'Are there going to be peaches this year?'

His grandfather was trying to draw him in with the good memories. He refused to be tempted. 'Not if you level the place.'

'That's true.' The wily old devil laughed wheezily. 'But then it's not my decision.' The laughter degenerated into a spasm of coughing. 'You always used to insist on picking the first one. Do you remember?'

'Yes, I remember.' He remembered being lifted up, cupping the velvety fruit in his hands. Clover and Rosie would love that, too, he thought. And Stacey. He wondered how it would feel to kiss her with the sweet juice on the her lips, feel her skin, warm from the sun, beneath his hand. And then he wondered if he was going crazy. 'Do you have to do this? Sell the place to developers?'

'You don't want me to? You can stop it any time you like.'

Yes. But only if he was prepared to play his grandfather's games. In his own way, the old man was just as manipulative as his father with his offers of a seat on the board. No amount of money would be enough for that.

His grandfather knew that only one thing would tempt him back to his childhood home: the walled garden where he'd spent so much of his time. But it was a honeypot. If he took it, like the fly, he'd be trapped.

'An industrial estate will spoil the view for the village,' he said.

'Maybe the residents of the village care more about having work locally than a view.' His grandfather wheeled his chair closer. 'Or maybe you're thinking about one villager in particular? Tell me, do those little girls still kick their ball over the wall?' Nash didn't answer. 'Their mother used to do a few hours for me when I was busy.'

'Did she?' Nash found himself wondering if she took the shortcut over the wall to work.

'She has green fingers up to her elbows. Have you seen her garden?'

'It doesn't take green fingers to grow weeds,' he said.

'A weed is only a flower growing in the wrong place. Stacey's garden is not the wrong place. If you've seen it, and you obviously have, you'll know that as well as I do.'

'She has some idea about growing wild flower

plants. As a business.' It was half a question. 'Is that a good idea?'

'Specialising is the only way for small concerns. Specialise and sell by mail order. Get on the internet.' Nash was aware of his grandfather's sharp eyes on him. His body might have let him down, but his mind was as sharp as it had ever been.

'That sounds a bit high-powered for Stacey.'

'She just needs someone to encourage her. Someone to give her confidence in herself. Her husband was killed a while back in a motor accident...maybe she told you?' Nash didn't confirm or deny it. 'It knocked the stuffing out of her for a while. Of course, she might just be glad of a job close to home—'

'She's talking about moving.'

'Ah.' That one thoughtful syllable held more knowledge of human nature than a book. 'Things must be bad, then. The house is a wreck, but she wouldn't leave her garden unless she had to.'

'It won't be easy to sell with an industrial estate on the other side of the wall.' It wouldn't be easy to sell, full stop. His grandfather was right. It needed a lot of work. The guttering was in a terrible state and he'd noticed a couple of loose tiles on the roof.

'Well, it's your choice.'

'I do the prodigal grandson bit or you'll sell the place to developers? Some choice. I'm a botanist, not a gardener.'

'You're running away, Nash. Burying yourself in some jungle is no life for a young man.'

'It certainly isn't a life for an old one,' he retaliated. 'And it will take more than a little moral black-mail to keep me here. If I leave, I won't ever be coming back, so why would I be worried about what you do with the place?' *If?* Until last week it hadn't been if, it had been when. *When* I leave…

'You love it. That's why.'

'Loved, Grandad. Loved.' It had been his refuge. The one place where no one ever had ever been angry… 'I'm not a kid any more. Besides, even if I wanted to, which I don't, I couldn't run a garden centre.'

'Pity. Gardening is the new sex, or so I've read in the newspapers.' Archie broke into a harsh spasm of coughing. 'It's a shame I'm too sick to take advantage of it,' he said, with a wry grin. Then, 'You could get someone else to run it for you.'

'What would be the point of that?'

'You tell me, lad. You're the one with a face like a wet weekend.' He glanced at the documents lying on the table beside him. 'Just tell me what you want and I'll do it. Stay or go. It's your decision.'

Yes, it was his decision and he should have made it last week, refused to allow himself to get bogged down in the emotion of the past. So why hadn't he? 'You should have given the land to my mother,' he said. 'She's your next of kin.'

'So she's fond of reminding me.' And he grinned. 'Once I've signed it over to you, I suppose there's nothing stopping you from doing just that. I promise you, *she* won't get sentimental over some old peach trees. Or the view.'

'I'm not… No.' His mother didn't know the

meaning of the word. 'You don't want me to do that, though, do you?'

He shrugged. As if it didn't matter. Nash wasn't fooled for a minute. 'So when are you leaving?'

'Not until Thursday. I've been asked to give a guest lecture at the university while I'm here. In fact they've asked me to take the new Chair in Botany.'

'Really?' If he'd hoped to impress the old man, he would have been disappointed. His grandfather simply picked up the papers and tucked them inside his dressing gown. 'In that case, these will keep,' he said. 'Come back when you've made up your mind. And bring a bottle of Scotch with you.'

'Are you allowed Scotch?'

'No. But don't worry, it'll have to stand in line to kill me.'

He stopped at the shop in the village, hoping to pick up some bread and milk. It was closed, but the card in the window caught his attention. *Room to Let— Suit Student. Apply Stacey O'Neill, The Lodge, Prior's Lane...*

So. She'd let him know, would she? He found himself grinning stupidly. There could be only two reasons why she hadn't told him that she had a room to let. She didn't trust him. Or she didn't trust herself. And he'd been on his very best behaviour, even when her eyes had been practically begging him to be on his worst.

Maybe he'd stop by and ask her which it was. Take her up on that invitation.

Of course he shouldn't. He knew he shouldn't. If

she'd been prepared to let him a room she would have said so when he'd asked. It wasn't as if he was serious about staying. It wouldn't be kind to embarrass her. It wouldn't be kind...

But to hell with being kind when he was spending his nights on the hard ground, tossing and turning with worry that her difficult-to-sell house would become impossible to sell if he robbed her of her view.

Besides, the thought of meeting the blushing Mrs O'Neill first thing in the morning, dishevelled from sleep, her hair mussed, her eyes not quite focussed and utterly vulnerable... Well, it was enough to give a man all kinds of straight-to-hell ideas.

He climbed astride his Harley and was halfway down Prior's Lane when he recalled that he was leaving on Thursday, right after that lecture. If he embarrassed Stacey into letting him her spare room, he knew he wouldn't be going anywhere for a very long time.

The ground might be hard, his sleeping bag lonely. But for a man who was determined to avoid complications, it was a whole lot safer.

Stacey, rubbing down the paintwork on the window, heard a motorcycle coming down the lane and for a moment, for just a moment, her heart turned over and she lifted her head to listen for that special note as the rider changed down, turned into the drive...

But the bike slowed before it reached the drive, slowed, turned, roared away. Just someone taking a wrong turning.

Once, the distant throb of a Harley would have been enough to reduce her to tears. Now she just carried on rubbing at the paint with the sandpaper. She'd loved Mike. Loved him a lot more than he'd loved her. He'd been a useless, serially unfaithful husband, and not much better as a father—she'd grown up; he hadn't—but she hadn't quite given up on him and for a long time she'd missed him. But her know-it-all sister was right. It was time to move on.

From her perch overlooking the garden, overlooking the garden wall, she saw Nash turn into the garden centre on a huge black motorcycle. She wasn't particularly surprised. Had it been him in the lane?

She leaned back, watched him unobserved for a moment as he unzipped his leathers. She remembered the scent—leather and hot oil and a man in the mood for love. He was the kind of man a woman could so easily lose her head over, she thought.

But no sane woman would put herself through that twice.

She glanced at the jam jar full of daisies she'd brought up to the bathroom to inspire her. Lawrence Fordham wouldn't bring her daisies, she thought. He was a traditional red rose man if ever there was one. And she was sure he wouldn't appreciate his date having hands that were rougher than his own. With a sigh, she reached for the rubber gloves.

Nash peeled off his leathers, took a beer from his coldbox, ripped off the ring pull and sat down on the edge of a raised bed to confront his choices. Instead he was confronted with the freshly weeded soft fruit garden.

After he'd cleared the base of the fruit trees, it had seemed only logical to keep going.

The pale globes of the gooseberries were a tender reminder of the tart Stacey had made and a blackbird was taking advantage of the rapidly ripening blackcurrants.

He'd told his grandfather that he wasn't a gardener, but he must have learned something as he'd trailed after the old man in what had always been his sanctuary, doing the little jobs he'd been entrusted with.

In fact, he realised, he'd learned a lot. Not just what to pull up and what to leave. When he'd got bored with pulling up the weeds, he'd looked at them, taken them apart to find out how they worked. He'd asked questions and his grandfather had always had time to tell him the answers.

Stay and this centuries-old garden would be his. There would be no strings attached, other than the moral imperative of his promise to look after the place.

But how could he do that if he was on the other side of the world?

In Central America he might find immortality. His name on some new miracle-working species of plant. Papers published in scientific journals. Listed alongside the great plant-hunters of the past. A week ago he'd been convinced that was all he desired.

A week ago he hadn't met Stacey.

Perhaps he should suggest that Archie give her the garden. She'd appreciate it, cherish it. There was nothing to stop him from giving it to her once the papers were signed. The idea was appealing. Hell, she could run her wild flower nursery from here...

Even as he was seized by the idea, he looked about him and took a reality check. It was a nice idea, but she had enough problems. Restoring and reglazing the greenhouses would be expensive. Of course there was no reason why he couldn't do that for her. There was no reason for him to rush off. He had all summer. He could refurbish the little office. Install a computer. Get someone to design her a website. Put a gate in the wall.

The idea took a hold, began to freewheel in his brain, and he took his beer and walked across to the nearest greenhouse.

It wasn't in such a bad way. Nothing that couldn't be put right in a few weeks. He kicked at a loose tile, lifted by the relentless force of a weed that had drifted in on the wind and settled in a muddy crack. He knelt and tugged it out. Tapped the tile back into place. Not bad at all. He sat back on his heels and thought about it. And gradually became aware of the faint plaintive mewing of the kittens.

Stacey wished she'd never started. She'd rather double-dig her vegetable garden than sandpaper wood. And this was the easy bit. Elbow grease, rather than skill.

Clover and Rosie had already deserted her. They'd started off full of enthusiasm but had quickly become bored. When they'd started making giant daisy chains from Nash's flowers, she knew shc'd lost their attention and sent them off to pick peas and pod them for tea.

She lifted the hem of her T-shirt and rubbed the sweat from her face. When she looked up, she saw that Nash had put a cardboard box on top of the wall, the sun gleaming pure gold from his shoulders as he hauled himself over and lifted it down. Did the man ever wear a T-shirt? Had he any idea of the effect his naked torso had on a woman?

She pulled a face. Of course he did. Mike would have walked around half-naked in the snow...

And after all she'd told the girls about the wall being unsafe, she thought crossly. It set such a bad example to have him hopping back and forth. If he wanted to come calling he'd better start putting on a shirt and coming to the front door like everyone else. She'd tell him so, too.

But not now. Now, she was too busy. Now, she was going to carry on rubbing at the woodwork and ignore him and whatever was in the box. He was just trying to get himself invited to tea again. Well, it wasn't going to work.

'Stacey.' He was standing beneath the window looking up at her, the box in his hands. 'Stacey!' he called again, refusing to be ignored.

'I'm busy, Nash. And if you've got more flowers in there, well, I'm running out of vases.'

'Not flowers. Look, can you come down? I've got a bit of a problem.' *He'd* got a problem! He should try her life for a day. 'I need your advice.'

Oh, sure! Did she look totally green?

She ignored him, but since he didn't wait for an answer, disappearing into the mud room beneath her, making himself totally at home, he was totally unaware of the fact.

The cheek of the man! Just because he'd fixed her lawn mower...just because she'd offered him a pre-dawn cup of tea...

She unwound herself from her awkward perch in the window and straightened her joints. By the time she reached the kitchen, Nash was not only inside, but helping himself to a bottle of milk from the fridge. 'What on earth do you think you're doing?' she demanded. Then she saw them. Three, no four little scraps of fur tucked into his T-shirt and mewing pitifully from the box.

'I'm sorry, but I didn't have any milk. Do you think I should warm it?'

'The milk?' She looked up. 'Where's their mother?'

'I don't know, but I haven't seen her since yesterday. I'll go and look for her in a minute, but these little things are desperately hungry. Should I warm the milk?' he repeated.

'Yes... No...' She pushed the strands of hair that had escaped the duck. 'Just take the chill off it.' She picked one of the kittens out of the box. It was ginger and white with a black smudge on its nose. 'Oh, sweetheart, you are so beautiful.'

'Mummy, did I see Nash…?' Clover tumbled into the kitchen with her basketful of peas, followed by Rosie. They came to a blushing halt as they saw him. Then they spotted the kittens. 'Oh, wow!'

Stacey exchanged a glance with Nash. Hers said, That's torn it… His said, I'm sorry, I didn't think… Mind-reading. That was a really bad sign…

'They're still very tiny,' she said, quickly. 'Do you think they can lap?'

'I don't know.' His mouth was smiling, his eyes were doing something else. Something that made her insides turn to marshmallow. 'I haven't asked them.'

Damn it! How dared he be cute? Waltzing in here with a box full of trouble. If they couldn't lap and their mother was lying dead in a ditch beside the main road, they'd die. And Rosie and Clover would be broken-hearted.

'Shall we find out?' she snapped, taking the milk from him, pouring it into a saucepan.

It took a while. A lot of dipping fingers in milk for the kittens to lick at, a lot of encouragement and spills as they climbed up onto the saucer before hunger and the basic instinct to survive kicked in and they got the hang of it.

Finally, they were satisfied, cleaned up and tucked back in the box where, exhausted, they immediately fell asleep. Nash looked at her. 'They'll make it, won't they?' he asked.

Play the
"LAS VEGAS" Game
and get
3 FREE GIFTS!

FREE GIFTS!

FREE GIFTS!

1. Pull back all 3 tabs on the card at right. Then check the claim chart to see what we have for you — 2 FREE BOOKS and a gift — ALL YOURS! ALL FREE!

2. Send back this card and you'll receive brand-new Harlequin Romance® novels. These books have a cover price of $3.50 each in the U.S. and $3.99 each in Canada, but they are yours to keep absolutely free.

3. There's no catch. You're under no obligation to buy anything. We charge nothing — ZERO — for your first shipment. And you don't have to make any minimum number of purchases — not even one!

4. The fact is, thousands of readers enjoy receiving their books by mail from the Harlequin Reader Service®. They enjoy the convenience of home delivery...they like getting the best new novels at discount prices, BEFORE they're available in stores...and they love their *Heart to Heart* newsletter featuring author news, horoscopes, recipes, book reviews and much more!

5. We hope that after receiving your free books you'll want to remain a subscriber. But the choice is yours — to continue or cancel, any time at all! So why not take us up on our invitation, with no risk of any kind. You'll be glad you did!

Visit us online at

www.eHarlequin.com

FREE!
No Obligation to Buy!
No Purchase Necessary!

Play the

"LAS VEGAS"
Game

PEEL BACK HERE ▶
PEEL BACK HERE ▶
PEEL BACK HERE ▶

YES! I have pulled back the 3 tabs. Please send me all the free Harlequin Romance® books and the gift for which I qualify. I understand that I am under no obligation to purchase any books, as explained on the back and opposite page.

386 HDL DC4R

186 HDL DC4H
(H-R-OS-05/01)

NAME	(PLEASE PRINT CLEARLY)

ADDRESS

APT.#	CITY

STATE/PROV.

ZIP/POSTAL CODE

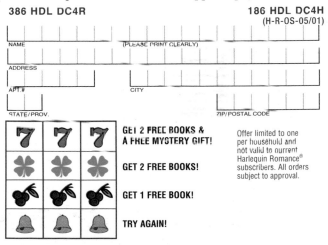

GET 2 FREE BOOKS & A FREE MYSTERY GIFT!

GET 2 FREE BOOKS!

GET 1 FREE BOOK!

TRY AGAIN!

Offer limited to one per household and not valid to current Harlequin Romance® subscribers. All orders subject to approval.

If offer card is missing write to: Harlequin Reader Service, 3010 Walden Ave., P.O. Box 1867, Buffalo, NY 14240-1867

BUSINESS REPLY MAIL
FIRST-CLASS MAIL   PERMIT NO. 717   BUFFALO, NY

POSTAGE WILL BE PAID BY ADDRESSEE

HARLEQUIN READER SERVICE
3010 WALDEN AVE
PO BOX 1867
BUFFALO NY 14240-9952

NO POSTAGE
NECESSARY
IF MAILED
IN THE
UNITED STATES

'Maybe. Whether I will is another matter altogether. I've got to go out tomorrow.' The hairdresser's in the morning. Archie. Lawrence in the evening. She hadn't even asked Vera if she'd babysit yet, either.

'They'll sleep most of the time, and I could look in on them, if you leave me a key.' A key? That was a pretty big step up from letting him walk into her kitchen unannounced. 'Or maybe you'd rather I took them back to the greenhouse?'

'No!' Not surprisingly, Rosie and Clover weren't having that.

'I suppose they'll be safer in here,' she agreed, reluctantly. 'If you really don't mind looking in on them.'

'Since I lumbered you with them, I'd better do my bit.' He grinned. 'Maybe I could offer you some soft fruit by way of payment for your hospitality?' Stacey just laughed. 'What?' She shook her head. 'There's a glut over there and I thought—'

'I know exactly what you thought. You thought maybe I'd make another pie and invite you to tea.'

'The idea never entered my head.'

'No?'

He looked affronted, which didn't fool her for a minute. After all, she could read his mind. 'But if you're asking, I wouldn't say no. You can't make pastry on an open fire.'

'Nash! I'm painting the bathroom. I don't have time for baking.'

'Are you? Oh, well, better forget it, then.' He

stood up quickly, so that she was confronted with those gorgeous thighs, a sight which momentarily robbed her of the power of speech even though her brain was screaming, Don't be an idiot…ask him to stay… He got as far as the door before he turned back. 'Unless…' He came back, couched down beside her again, looked her straight in the eyes. That wasn't fair. That was taking advantage… 'How would it be if you made some pastry while I took a shift with the decorating?'

He could decorate the bathroom, decorate the hall, decorate whatever he damned well pleased, if he kept looking at her with those smokey blue eyes. Paint her, even. All over with that lovely saffron-yellow silk emulsion… She slammed the brakes on her imagination.

'I thought you had something important to do today.' She'd meant to sound firm, but her voice hadn't caught up yet. It was still in dreamland, with the paint.

'It's done. I'm all yours.' She didn't doubt it for a moment. She was getting the message loud and clear. He would be all hers until the attraction of her pastry waned before some new temptation and he moved on.

She could read him like a book, but she still said, 'You're sure?'

'A couple of hours' painting in return for a couple of hours' cooking? It sounds like a good deal to me.'

'It's more than a couple of hours. I'm still at the rubbing-down stage.'

'Rubbing-down's my favourite job,' he said, with a perfectly straight face. Oh, crumbs. What on earth had she agreed to? More importantly, what did he think she'd agreed to? He straightened, stretched out his hand to help her up. Her hand slipped into his like cold fingers into a warm mitten. Pure heaven. 'Why don't you show me what you want me to do?' He pulled her to her feet.

Speechless in the face of such temptation, she allowed him to keep her hand and, without a word, led the way upstairs.

It was all sloping ceilings and oak beams. Bags of character, but Nash suspected it hadn't been seriously harassed by a paintbrush in years. Stacey had started to rub down the woodwork, but apart from that she hadn't made much impression.

'What are you going to do with it?'

'P-paint it,' Stacey said, when she managed to unglue her mouth. 'It's going to be yellow and white. Like the daisies.'

The flowers were lying in a tangled heap of oversized daisy chain. Clover and Rosie's idea of helping, he suspected. He picked them up while Stacey explained what she planned to do. How she'd bought some tiles. Something about a blind. One of them had been fastened into a circle, a chaplet, a fairy crown, and he held it in both hands.

She looked at the flowers nervously, then at him. 'Look, you've got more than enough on your plate next door, Nash. You don't have to do this... honestly...'

'Sure I do.' And he lifted the daisy chain crown and laid on her head. She made a grab for it, but he caught her wrist in his hand and stopped her tearing it off. 'Leave it,' he said. 'It's perfect. You're perfect.' And he put his other arm around her waist and pulled her into his body and did what he'd been wanting to do since he'd first set eyes on her. He ditched 'sensible' and 'wise' and a whole lot of other words he'd been hiding behind for too long, consigning them to the wastebin of life, and he kissed her. Hard and sweet.

CHAPTER SEVEN

STACEY was going to protest. The minute she regained possession of her mouth, she was going to tell Nash Gallagher that this was taking unfair advantage. Softening her heart with helpless little kittens, earning her undying gratitude by offering to make a start on the bathroom, then, when her defences were down, kissing her.

Really. Except her mouth was entirely occupied as Nash began to take untold liberties with it and his tongue, teasing against her lips, invited her willing participation in this sweet seduction.

Well, she wouldn't participate. This was not what she wanted. At least, it was, but she had made up her mind to be sensible...that she wouldn't do this...absolutely, definitely not... No matter how great the temptation... And she reached up to grab his shoulder, to make it clear that she wanted him to stop what he was doing right now.

Beneath her palm his skin was sensuously silky and her hand softened against his warmth, curled into the curve of his powerful neck.

He released her wrist and for a moment she thought he was going to let her go, but she definitely didn't want that, either. Not *right now*...

Stacey might be confused but fortunately Nash seemed to know what he was doing, because he wrapped his other arm about her in a way that suggested she wouldn't be going anywhere for a very long time.

Well, so long as one of them knew what they were doing, Stacey thought, she could worry about being sensible later.

Her traitorous lips were way ahead of her, eagerly parting beneath his tender onslaught. And the rest of her was catching up fast.

It had been years, but her memory didn't let her down. It had been working towards this moment ever since she'd backed out of the strawberry bed, taking her on tantalising trailers of the slam-dunk of desire, hot and sweet and urgent.

But the trailers were done, the adverts over. This was the main feature and she was fast approaching the boneless stage, the point at which melt-down seemed certain, inevitable, unavoidable. Then Nash stopped kissing her, drew back a little and she heard herself make a tiny mew of protest as for a moment he just looked at her, his eyes smoking with reflected heat...

'Have you ever—?' he began, then stopped as if to catch his breath. She could feel his heart pounding beneath her breast, feel the swift rise and fall of his chest as his breath came in ragged gasps, like her own. She wanted to lay her head against it, feel the heat, relish the need, yet something warned her that what he was saying was important .

'What? Have I ever...what?'

'Have you ever,' he began again, his voice thick,

soft as old velvet, 'have you ever tasted a peach
straight from the tree?'

Whatever she'd expected, it hadn't been that and,
confused, she leaned away from him to look up into
his face, to read what was hidden behind the words.
Behind him, Clover was standing in the doorway, a
tiny kitten curled up in her hand, her eyes narrowed
thoughtfully.

Oh, hell! What had she seen? What was she thinking? 'Clover—' she began, her mind freewheeling
frantically, trying to catch a gear and say something...anything... 'What are you doing with that
kitten?'

'He was awake. I think he's hungry again.' Then,
'Is Nash going to be my new daddy?'

There was a painfully long silence before Stacey
managed a laugh, pushed his arm from her waist.
Nash made no move to stop her. Heck, he was probably trying to decide between making a dash for the
stairs, or whether it would wiser to take the more
direct route and risk the jump from the bathroom
window, just a step away and invitingly open.

'New daddy?' she repeated, unable to look at him.

'He was kissing you. Daddy kissed you like that.'

Poor man. One kiss and her daughter had a shot-
gun at his back. 'Oh, yes, well, I was just, um, feeling a bit sad, about the kittens losing their mummy,'
she improvised. 'Nash was trying to cheer me up.'
And succeeding. Definitely succeeding. She'd quite
forgotten about their little orphans.

Clover didn't look convinced. Well, she was
nearly ten years old, quite old enough to understand

the difference between being cheered up and being kissed senseless. 'When Sarah Graham's mother was cheered up like that,' she said, knowingly, 'Sarah had a new daddy *and* a baby sister.'

Oh, great. She finally looked at Nash, hoping for a little assistance. Instead, he reached out and ran a fingertip lightly over the back of the kitten.

'Would you like a baby sister?' he asked Clover.

Oh, that was a big help.

Clover didn't let her down, though. 'No way,' she said, without hesitation. 'I've got a little sister and she's a real pain.' Stacey's sigh of relief came a fraction of a second too soon. 'I'd wouldn't mind a baby brother, though. Like Harry. He's my cousin.'

Not like Harry, Stacey thought, with his dark curls. But a baby boy with skin like sunshine and hair the colour of clotted cream... 'Clover, take that kitten downstairs right now and put him in the box with the others,' she said, rather sharply. 'And then wash your hands. With soap and hot water.'

'Okay.' Clover made a move, but didn't get further than the door. 'Where is the mummy cat?' she asked Nash. Stacey sensed he was looking at her and she wasn't sure she wanted to see the expression in his eyes. Total panic, probably. But he was waiting for her lead, a hint on how she planned to deal with the missing cat. 'She might be hurt,' Clover went on, before she could think of anything. Coherent thought was not easy when you'd been caught necking like some giddy teenager by your nine-year-old daughter. 'You should be looking for her.'

'Clover, darling,' Stacey began, gently, thinking of all the small accident victims she saw every time she cycled into town on the busy main road.

'She might not be dead!'

'You're right, Clover,' Nash said, quickly. 'I'll go and look for her. In fact, I intended to do that as soon as I was sure the kittens were all right.'

That was it, then. He didn't need the bathroom window; her daughter had offered him a more gracious exit. 'Yes, do go,' Stacey urged him. 'I can handle the bathroom.'

'Can you?' His mouth lifted at one corner in an almost smile that mocked both of them. 'Does that mean I lose out on the pie?'

'Too much pastry is bad for you.'

'Is that right?' He shrugged. 'I wouldn't know.' No. He'd said. Pastry and camp fires were mutually exclusive. 'But don't let the fruit go to waste.' He didn't wait for her thanks, just ruffled Clover's tawny curls and headed for the stairs.

Stacey picked up the sandpaper as if it were a lifeline and, since her legs were apparently made of marshmallow, she abandoned all ambition to remain on her feet and set to work on the skirting board.

That way she wouldn't be tempted to look out of the window down into the walled garden where Nash was starting his search for the cat. And she wasn't picking fruit. She wasn't going over that wall ever again. Ever.

'Mummy! Mummy!' She gradually became aware of Rosie's insistent little voice and turned away from the window. 'Where's Nash going?'

That was easy. 'He's going to look for the kittens' mummy.'

'Oh, right. Then he'll come back later, won't he?'

Impossible to answer. If he found the mother cat. If he even looked for her. 'I don't know. It might take him a while.' Possibly for ever.

Damn, damn, damn. He hadn't meant to do that. Hadn't meant to kiss her. It was crazy. He didn't want to be that involved, caught up in a tangle of emotional commitments.

Alone, no one could hurt him. That was the tenet he had lived by since he was old enough to understand the games that men and women played, the strategies they used to wound one another. It had served him well enough. Until now.

He dropped to his haunches and leaned back against the warm brick of the wall, fear clawing at his insides as he reckoned how far he had strayed from 'alone' in a few short days.

It was easy to be alone when you'd never wanted anything else. Easy to keep your eyes fixed on the narrow path ahead when there was no one to distract you, no one to make you yearn to linger in the by-ways.

But what did you do when your body was on fire, when it was demanding that you stop running and promising you that you wouldn't be sorry? You didn't believe it. Not if you had any sense.

But what did you do when something that might have been your heart was urging you to wrap yourself in the warmth of a woman's arms and in return give her and her children all that you had? Give her the baby boy her eyes told you she longed for? When it suddenly seemed the most important thing in the world?

You suffered. That was what you did.

You felt angry and helpless. Acknowledged the sudden yawning emptiness in a life that had, until a few days ago, been running on smoothly oiled lines. Like an express train heading for the big city.

Then a ball had come flying over the wall, switching the points, sending him down one of those little country branch lines. Another moment in Stacey's arms and he might never have noticed until it was too late. Or, if he'd noticed, he might not have cared.

Nash pushed himself up and away from the wall. It was time he stopped wallowing in sentimentality and began thinking with his head again. He was leaving on Thursday. He'd be away for at least a year. He didn't have time for this. He had to forget all about sweet peaches and warm lips and the kind of loving that haunted his deepest dreams.

He was going to find that damned cat, bury it, and get out of here as fast as he knew how.

Stacey, determined not to think about Nash, wielded the sandpaper with ferocity for all of twenty minutes. Then she checked on the kittens. Then she made a cup of tea. Then she thought about all that lovely soft fruit on the other side of the wall. It was all very well saying she wouldn't go over there, but it would be a criminal waste to leave it to be crushed by a nasty great bulldozer.

Help yourself, he'd said. Don't let it go to waste.

He was very free with it, considering he was just clearing the place up. Still. He was right. Vera would be more than happy to have a couple of homemade pies for her freezer in return for looking after the girls on Monday night. And when he came back…if he came back…Nash would be hungry.

She clambered over the wall, picked enough fruit to fill half a dozen pies. And when there was no more fruit left to pick she still lingered, hoping he'd come back and find her there. One kiss, and common sense had taken a hike.

She wandered along the newly weeded paths. The raised beds had been cleared and were ready for planting. The lavender and the going-to-seed herbs had been cut back. The garden was beginning to look the way it had when Archie had been running the place, selling his lovely perennial plants to the people clever enough to find him. Mostly giving away the glut of fruit and vegetables he grew.

It was no way to run a business, she'd told him. He'd said he didn't need much.

What on earth was going on?

If this was all going to be bulldozed, why on earth was Nash bothering to tidy it up like this? And why would one man be clearing it, anyway? A machine could rip through this in a few hours.

She suddenly had more questions than answers, but Nash didn't come back and she had a glut of fruit to clean.

By the time she'd finished her hands were stained red with juice, her fingernails black. With any luck,

Lawrence Fordham would take one look at her when he came to pick her up tomorrow night and run. With any luck, he'd tell Dee that he'd rather die celibate than take her sister to the firm's dinner on Saturday.

Still Nash hadn't come back.

She eventually prised the girls away from the kittens, into the bath and finally to bed. And then she stretched out in what was left of the hot water. Four inches if she wanted it hot. Five inches warm. Six inches tepid. The alternative was to wait for the economy rate electricity to kick in some time after midnight.

She settled for warm, and after a quick soak took a scrubbing brush to her hands. They were still pink when the water began to feel distinctly chilly, but that just might have been the friction. She didn't care much, but fell into bed and an exhausted sleep.

It took him hours to find the mother cat. He walked a mile towards town, searching both sides of the road, up one side, back the other. Then he walked a mile in the other direction, back beyond the village. Then he collected his torch and started exploring the farm tracks. She might be dead, but he couldn't bear the thought of her lying somewhere in pain.

He'd just about given up hope when the beam of light had been reflected in the cat's pain-filled eyes and he found her, caught up on some wire, but still clinging to life.

*　　*　　*

Stacey was woken by small stones being tossed up at her window. At first she couldn't make out what it was.

Then another stone clipped against the window and she climbed out of bed and peered down into the garden.

'Nash?' If he thought he could creep back in the middle of the night when the girls were asleep—

'Stacey, I've got the cat.'

'She's alive?'

'Of course she's alive,' he hissed. Yes, well, he would hardly have brought her the body. 'For God's sake, let me in, will you.' She offered him a silent apology as she flew downstairs, unbolting the back door with shaking fingers. 'The vet's stitched her up and given her antibiotics.' Staring at the poor creature, wrapped in a blanket, half doped but still mewing plaintively, she couldn't believe the vet hadn't kept her in the surgery overnight. 'He said she'd do better if she knew her kittens were safe.'

'Oh, Nash!' She'd never been a pretty cat, but with swathes of her fur shaved away and the black rows of stitches holding her together, she looked like something put together by a feline Frankenstein. 'Where did you find her?'

'On the lane leading up to Bennett's Farm. She was caught up in some barbed wire.'

'But that's miles!' As he stepped into the kitchen she saw that his own hands and arms hadn't escaped unscathed from the wire, or the cat's claws. 'What about you? Shouldn't you have a tetanus shot, or something?'

'Don't worry, I'm up to date.' He put the cat into the box with her babies and they both watched for a moment as she licked at them, reassuring herself that they were all there and safe.

'Come on,' Stacey said, after a while. 'Up to date or not, we'd better clean up those scratches.' She found a bottle of antiseptic and poured some in a bowl, then topped it up with lukewarm water from the kettle.

'I washed them at the surgery,' he protested. 'And the wire was clean.'

'Really?' She found some cottonwool, then turned to him. 'But was it sterilised?'

He finally smiled. 'That I couldn't guarantee.'

'I thought not.' Taking hold of his wrist, she began to gently swab at the scratches. 'Lord, but this must have hurt.'

'I'll live.' With her cool fingers around his wrist, her hair mussed from bed, brushing against his chin, Nash thought he might do more than that. He thought he might fly.

Above the sharp scent of the antiseptic, Stacey smelt tantalisingly of clean sheets and toothpaste. More appealing than any exotic perfume. As she stopped to hook her hair back behind her ear and bent over his arm to concentrate on her task, Nash decided that the last few hours would have been worth it just for this.

'Are you hungry?' she asked, glancing up at him. Yes, he was hungry. He was so empty that the pain of it gnawed at him. But it wasn't food he needed. It was Stacey. Right now. In his arms. 'Have you eaten?'

It was ridiculous. He didn't need anyone. He'd never needed anyone. 'No. But I've got—'

'Eggs?'

'Stacey—'

'It's all right, I get them in exchange for my vegetables. They're organic, free-range,' she explained.

'Your vegetables?'

'What? Oh…no…' She was tipping the water down the sink, and turned, grinning. 'Well, you have to keep a close eye on the runner beans. Scrambled?'

She was talking too much. She knew it. She always did that when she was nervous. And she was nervous. Because she'd decided that Nash wasn't going anywhere. He was staying with her…

'Stacey, it's late. I'd better go. If you can manage.'

He checked the cat, more to avoid looking at her than for any other reason. Looking at her was doing something to his insides. Making him feel stuff he didn't want to feel. He didn't want to be this vulnerable. Hated this need for her that was gnawing at him…

She knelt down beside him. The cat was half asleep, purring quietly now, the kittens curled up against her belly. Safe. Warm.

'Stacey…' She turned to look at him. He'd been going to tell her that he was leaving. That on Thursday he'd be gone. The words died on his lips and instead he reached for her, laying his hand against her cheek...

'Stacey!'

She jumped guiltily and spun round, leapt to her feet. 'Dee...'

'I brought the car round. I was going to put the key through the letter-box but when I saw the light on I thought there must be something wrong.'

'No. At least, yes.' Stacey swallowed, feeling as guilty as a teenager caught kissing the local bad boy by her mother. It was all she could do to stop herself tugging down her thigh-length nightie. She really should have stopped to pull on her jogging pants. 'We've got a casualty,' she said. 'A cat.'

'A cat?' Dee's eyes were fixed on Nash. 'But you don't have a cat.'

'No. She lives at Archie's place. The old garden centre. She's, um, had kittens. Would you like one for Harry?'

'No, I wouldn't. And since when did kittens constitute an emergency?' Dee didn't even glance at the box; her attention was entirely fixed upon the man crouched beside the box.

Nash straightened. 'They don't. It was the barbed wire that caused the problem.'

'And you are?' Oh, God, Stacey thought. Dee was doing her lady of-the-manor impression.

'Nash Gallagher.' He extended his hand; it was ignored.

'Nash is working next door,' Stacey said, quickly. 'Clearing the site.'

'Clearing the site? You mean he's a labourer?'

'Dee!'

He touched her arm gently, reassuringly. 'It's all right, Stacey. It's not something I need to apologise for.' He turned to Dee. 'Yes, ma'am, I've been labouring in Archie's garden.' Then he smiled. 'Stacey's been kind enough to provide the occasional cup of tea. And take in some motherless kittens.'

'I don't doubt it. She's always had a weakness for small helpless creatures. And men with muscles.'

Stacey groaned in silent mortification. Forget lady-of-the-manor, Dee sounded exactly like her mother the day she'd first encountered Mike. Come to think of it, dressed to slay the opposition in an aggressively cut business suit and with heels high enough to skewer anyone inclined to disagree with her, Dee looked a lot like their mother.

'Nash,' she said, quickly, 'this is my sister, Dee Harrington. She's on her way to the airport.' She hoped that Dee would take the hint and go.

'Ms Harrington,' he murmured, acknowledging the woman who had just stopped him from making the biggest mistake of his life. He knew he should be grateful, but he couldn't quite bring himself to offer her his hand again.

She nodded without any obvious warmth and then waited for him to go. For a moment common sense warred with the desire to explain that labouring wasn't what he did for a living, to tell her exactly who he was. Common sense won. 'I'll leave you to it, Stacey,' he said, heading for the door.

'But I thought you were going to have some breakfast.'

'Another time.' Let Ms Harrington make of that what she would. As if it was any of her business. 'If you need anything, you know where I am.'

'And just where is that?' Dee hissed as the door closed behind him.

Stacey pushed her hair back. 'I told you, he's working at the garden centre—'

'That wasn't what I asked.'

No. It wasn't. 'He's camping out there, if you must know.'

'And he makes a habit of calling in the middle of the night with injured animals?'

'No!' Dee's only response was to lift her eyebrows. 'He brought the kittens and then went to find their mother. She's been hurt, Dee. Badly hurt. It took him hours to find her and he's just brought her back from the vet.'

'At four o'clock in the morning?'

Stacey was getting seriously tired of Dee's big sister act. 'I don't suppose the cat can tell the time.'

'You haven't learned a thing, have you?'

'Please, Dee—'

'I can't believe it. He's exactly like Mike. All brawn and no brain. Zero ambition. There was some excuse when you were a kid—'

'He's not like that at all. He's a—' About to say that Nash was a botanist, a doctor of philosophy, some inner sense of self-preservation saved her. But he wasn't a bit like Mike. Well, maybe physically, just a bit, and she could see why Dee might assume the rest. But they weren't alike in any way that mattered. 'It's not like that, Dee.'

'The hell it isn't. I saw the way you were looking at him. I saw the way he was looking at you. Don't do it,' she warned.

'I haven't!' But she blushed as she remembered the way she'd responded to his kiss. Responded and then some.

'No? He's a stud, Stacey. He's just out for some summer fun with you, and I don't doubt it will be fun, but what then? He'll be gone. And you're a mother. You've got responsibilities.'

This was too close to her own reasoning to argue with. 'You're overreacting. Honestly. Nothing's happened.' One kiss. What was one kiss? One kiss too many, that was what it was.

She couldn't have been convincing because Dee put her hand on her shoulder. 'Please, Stacey. Listen to me. I can see the attraction. I'm not made of stone, but think about it. Even if he stays, what kind of future would you have? You'll just be starting over again from the same place you were when you married Mike. With a man on the fast track to nowhere. Only this time you'll be thirty.'

'Twenty-eight,' she said, fed up with the rising thirty argument. She was twenty-eight for two more weeks. That wasn't old. And she had a whole year before she was thirty. 'You're overreacting. Honestly. He's leaving in a day or two and I'm going out with Lawrence tomorrow night. Tonight,' she said, quickly correcting herself. 'Tonight,' she repeated. She considered adding how much she was looking forward to Saturday, too, but, doubting her ability to be convincing, she thought better of it.

'Yes. Please make an effort, Stacey,' Dee said, wearily, dropping the car keys on the table. 'Tim's waiting for me; I've got to go. I suggest you get back to bed. You need all the beauty sleep you can get.'

Well, thanks, sis. I really needed that, Stacey thought. She said, 'Have a good time in Paris.'

'I'm not going to have a good time, Stacey. I'm going to work. Some of us take life seriously, you know. Maybe it's time you stopped wasting your life day-dreaming and tried it. Work out what you want. Maybe it isn't Lawrence, but you've got to have a goal in life. Before you met Mike you had a brain. Why don't you plug it back in and see if it's still in working order?'

CHAPTER EIGHT

WELL, Stacey thought, in the silence following her sister's departure, that told her. In fact there'd been a surfeit of advice coming her way in the last twenty-four hours. Most of it conflicting. Don't give up on your dreams. Dump them. Get a grip. Take control. Reach for the moon.

From her bedroom, she saw the faint glimmer of light from beyond the garden wall and thought about her dreams. But Nash would be moving on in a day or two. Maybe it was time she did that, too.

Maybe she should make a list. Dee was very hot on lists. Maybe she should write down what was really important to her. The small things. The big things. The utterly impossible. The totally stupid.

Okay, so it was four in the morning and she needed all the beauty sleep she could get, but it was getting light and she was wide awake. She could go and prick out a load more seedlings. Or she could spend the time putting her life in order.

The seedlings sounded the more attractive proposition, but she fished around in the muddle of her bedside cabinet and found a notebook she'd bought to record those wonderful thoughts that only came in the middle of the night.

She opened it for the first time in months, wondering what ground-breaking ideas had come to her in the wee small hours.

Eat more rice and pasta. She'd thought that was important enough to write down in the middle of the night?

Check the greenhouse for slugs last thing every night. She remembered that one. She'd been dreaming about walking into the greenhouse and finding nothing but bare stalks...

But after that it went downhill, with nothing more positive than a reminder to order extra milk. She tore the pages out and on a new page she wrote a big heading—LIFE PLAN.

1. Have sex with Nash Gallagher before he moves on.

Okay, so that was firmly in the totally stupid category. But it was her first thought, which had to be revealing.

2. Keep my house.

3. Finish the bathroom so that I can let a room and keep my house.

4. Let a room, so that I can keep my house.

5. Marry Lawrence Fordham, but only if he moves in with me so that I can keep my house.

6. Start my own wild flower nursery.

She stopped then, because things were beginning to get serious, and stared at the list. At some point she would have to cross out the two utterlies. The utterly stupid and the utterly impossible. Now would be as good a time as any. She put a line through numbers one and five.

That just left her with the bathroom tiling, an urgent need for a lodger, an absolute determination not to leave her house and an acknowledgement that dreams won't go away, no matter how unattainable they might seem, or how much they were put down by a big sister.

Which was why she reinstated the utterly stupid before going to check on her feline guests.

'Is it safe to come in?'

Stacey quickly shut her notebook on lists that had assumed epic, epic proportions since the early hours. Just the sound of his voice was sufficient to cause a major tremor in the pit of her stomach, a tremor that conflicted with her newly minted life plan—to keep her feet firmly grounded while she reached for the moon.

She did her best to ignore it and looked up. The feet, she discovered, weren't that firmly grounded. Just a smile from Nash Gallagher was sufficient to have a warm flush of longing heating her skin and leave her floating a couple of inches above the quarry tiled floor.

'Safe? Why wouldn't it be?' she asked. The voice was supposed to be light, friendly. She might have temporarily wavered on the 'stupid' issue in the early hours, but she'd whipped her hormones back into line.

Nash pushed a lock of floppy hair back from his forehead, putting a severe strain on her willpower. 'Your sister disapproved of my middle-of-the-night visit,' he said, his eyes crinkling into a smile that invited her laugh, too. 'I thought she might have left a watch dog to keep you from temptation.'

Oh, so he thought he was irresistible, did he? Yes, well. He could be right. 'I think it would be safe to say that Dee would disapprove of you at any time of the day.' Dee was undoubtedly right. Nash Gallagher was nothing but trouble. Knowing that did not make resistance to his all too obvious charms any easier. 'But you're safe enough; she's in Paris this morning. She was on her way to the airport when she stopped by to leave me her car.'

'Will she be gone long?' he enquired, hopefully.

'Sorry, it's just an overnight trip. There's been a hiccup in her yoghurt strategy, apparently.' His brows quirked dramatically. 'She's the sales director for Fordham Foods.'

'Is she? Well, I can't say I'm surprised.'

'No.' Stacey shrugged. 'She's the brainy one.' While I just drool over brawn, Stacey thought, as she handed him her spare back door key, holding it carefully by the end so that their fingers wouldn't touch. They touched anyway, and all kinds of dangerous urges warred with hard-won reason. Taking care not to quite meet his gaze, which she could feel burning into her skin to reinforce the tingle left by the briefest of touches, she snatched her hand away. 'I—I've moved the cat into the mud room. She's been fed and she's got a litter tray. It's happy families in there.' She hadn't been sure if he'd remember his promise to look in on them and had been planning to ask Vera to pop round during the day, but this was easier. Too easy. Falling in lust should be made a great deal more difficult. 'If you can just look in on her once in a while. I'll be back before the girls come out of school.'

'You're going to be out all day?'

'I don't have my sister's car very often, so I have to make the most of it. Why? Did you want something?'

His eyes told her exactly what he wanted. But his mouth said, 'I was going to take you up on those eggs you promised me.'

'Oh, sure, help yourself,' she said. 'You'll find them in the pantry.' They both knew that wasn't what he'd meant, but she gathered her bag and keys and headed for the door before she was offering him breakfast in bed. In the bright light of day, with her girls chattering around her as they'd fought over breakfast, she'd crossed through the 'utterly stupid' dream once and for all. Utterly stupid was definitely off the agenda. Besides, she had a date with a beautician and Nash was right about her sister: if she missed her appointment, Dee would not be amused. 'There's tea in the pot, if you want some.'

'Stacey.' She was at the door, nearly safe. 'If you have to go out now, maybe we could do something this evening.' *Something?* What kind of something? She reined in her wildest dreams. 'How would it be if I got a takeaway and came round later?' *Later?* Was he asking her out? Or, rather, asking her to stay in. With him. On a date. 'After you've put Clover and Rosie to bed,' he added, so that she could be absolutely clear the way his mind was working.

Life, she thought, was not fair. But perhaps life, like her sister, was trying to tell her something. 'I'm sorry, Nash, but I'm going out tonight.'

'Out?' He sounded distinctly jealous and her hormones began to yap pathetically. She refused to encourage him to be jealous. It was a negative feeling.

'It's nothing exciting. A town-twinning thing in Maybridge.' She desperately wanted to tell him that she'd much rather stay in and share a takeaway with him, but there was no future in it. 'Maybe another time.' They both knew that another time was not going to happen, and she'd be happier not knowing what she'd be missing when he moved on.

'I really wanted to thank you for saving me from blood poisoning.'

'I'd have done it for anyone,' she said. Not kind. But then she wasn't feeling particularly kind. She was feeling thoroughly frustrated. She'd been a widow for three years and not once in all that time had she met a man who could raise her blood pressure by a single point. Now, just one look from Nash and it was threatening to blast the machine apart. It was so hard to leave him. Walk away. But she had to think of her life plan. She'd blown it once before on a man who had done unspeakable things to her blood pressure. Twice would be stupid. 'There's a pie in the fridge,' she said. Well, she'd been standing there too long not to say something. 'Help your-self.'

He frowned. 'Stacey, have I done something wrong? Yesterday—'

'Yesterday was…' She caught at her breath. 'Well, yesterday.' She glanced at her watch rather than meet his eyes. 'I'm sorry but I have to go, Nash, or I'll be late.' And she closed the door quickly.

Nash watched her go. Walk past the window. She was walking away from him. Well, it was what he wanted, wasn't it? No commitments. He poured himself a cup of tea. Fried a panful of eggs. Cleared up. Checked the cat.

He was about to let himself out when there was a ring at the front doorbell.

'Is this The Lodge?' The girl couldn't have been more than nineteen or twenty. She was smoothly pretty with glossy highlighted hair, unlived-in skin and knowing eyes. 'I heard there was a room to let. I do hope it hasn't gone.' Everything about her invited flirtation, and he'd never been one to turn down that kind of party. But he didn't respond to the quick flare of interest, the ready smile. He wanted Stacey, not some girl who hadn't got so much as a laughter line around her eyes. Her smile suggested he invite her in to look around. 'I'm a bit desperate.'

'I'm sorry, I can't help you. You'll have to come back when Mrs O'Neill is home. About four o'clock.' She'd have to be back when Rosie and Clover came home from school.

'Can I leave my number? Maybe you could give me a call?'

He didn't think she was talking about the room, but he shrugged and took the piece of paper she gave him and glanced at it. 'I'll pass it on.'

Then he shut the door and wondered how on earth he was going to spend the rest of the day without Stacey within calling distance.

Stacey had her facial, her curls put in restraints and her hands and nails pampered, then, when she'd been thoroughly polished, she called in at the bank to see how they felt about loaning her the money to start a wild flower nursery.

The hair, or maybe it was the manicure, seemed to help, because the manager didn't actually laugh. He wasn't exactly enthusiastic, either, but he did give her a pile of leaflets on starting a business and told her to come back and see him when she had a business plan. A life plan wasn't enough, apparently.

She had a sandwich in town and then drove out to visit Archie. He was looking frail, but seemed pleased to see her. 'Have you come into money, girl?' he asked, as she bent to kiss his cheek.

'No, more's the pity. Why?'

'Well, you haven't come on your bike,' he said. 'Not looking like that.'

'Oh, no. I've got my sister's car for the day.'

'Damn. I was hoping you'd got a new man in your life.'

'Then I'm sorry to disappoint you,' she said, putting down the treats she'd brought him.

'Young men are so slow to spot a good thing these days. I'd have snapped up a pretty young widow like you, given half the chance. Still would, given a bit of encouragement.' His dry laugh turned into a cough. 'Yes, well. Maybe I'm kidding myself. So, how's my garden doing?'

'Actually it's looking pretty good.'

'Oh?' His head came up and Stacey saw the sudden spark of interest.

'Do you want to tell me what's going on, Archie? Am I getting light industry as a neighbour, or is that just gossip?'

'Gossip?'

'I checked at the Planning Office and they've approved planning permission for industrial units.' His silence implied agreement. 'So why is someone taking the trouble to clear the paths, weed the fruit garden and generally put things back the way they were when you were looking after the place?'

'Is that what's happened?' His lined face creased into a smile. 'Well, well, well.'

'You know all about it, don't you? What's going on?'

'You're worried about having industry next door?'

'I'm not wildly happy about it. But it's more than that. If the garden centre is going to reopen, I'd like to know. I'm looking for a commercial outlet, Archie. I've decided to go for it…the wild flower nursery.'

'You'd like to rent the place, is that it?'

'I think that's a bit ambitious. But if I could come to some kind of arrangement—'

'There's nothing wrong with ambition. If you're going commercial you'll need the space, larger greenhouses. But I'm sorry, Stacey, it's nothing to do with me. You'd have to ask whoever's working there. What's his name?'

'Gallagher. Nash Gallagher.' She waited, but he didn't noticeably react to the name. Well, maybe his smile might have deepened a little, but it was difficult to tell. 'And I did ask him. He just said he was clearing the place up.' Which he was. 'Can I ask you who you sold the garden to? So I can find out what's happening.'

'I haven't sold it, Stacey.'

'But—'

An orderly appeared at his side and nodded to Stacey as he released the brakes on his wheelchair. 'Visiting time's over, Archie. Time for your bath.'

'Go and see Mr Gallagher again. Ask him what he's really doing there, then come back and tell me what he says,' the old man called out as he was wheeled away.

She didn't understand. If Archie hadn't sold the garden...

Oh, damn. He'd once told her that he'd been gardening up at the big house all his life and she'd got the impression that he'd been given the kitchen garden in lieu of a pension when the estate was sold up. He'd never been exactly bothered about making a profit.

But he must have had it on some peppercorn rent. After all, twenty years ago, garden centres weren't big business. And twenty years ago the owners would never have got planning permission for anything more industrial than a potting shed.

It would seem that poor Archie didn't know any more than she did.

The sweat was running down his face, but it was nearly done. Nash opened a bottle of water, drank a few mouthfuls, then tipped some over his head. He could hear the excited little voices of Rosie and Clover as they raced in from school, eager to see the kittens.

'Mummy, is Nash coming over for tea tonight?' Rosie, said as she cradled the kitten.

How quickly they'd got used to him, Stacey thought. Expected him to be there. She was right not to get any more involved. She could handle heartache; she was used to it. They'd had more than enough in their little lives. Even after just a few days they'd miss him when he moved on.

'Not tonight. I'm going out, remember? I told you.'

'Do you have to?'

'You'll have fun. Vera's coming to sit with you. She says she's got a new Disney film you'll enjoy.'

'Well, maybe Nash could come and watch it, too.'

Vera would certainly enjoy that, Stacey thought as she ran upstairs to change out of her going-to-town clothes, tugging the sticky shirt out of her waistband and undoing the buttons, balling it ready to toss into the laundry basket as she went. She flung open the bathroom door and came to an abrupt halt.

It was yellow. The wonderful deep yellow that echoed the heart of the ox-eye daisies Nash had picked for her. And the woodwork was petal-white, with not a streak or a run...

Nash had turned as she opened the door and was waiting for some comment. Difficult, when she was speechless... 'Nash, it's wonderful. I didn't expect... You didn't have to...'

'I know.' He seemed riveted to the spot. Then he swallowed and said, 'But it was a very good pie.'

'Was it?' Oh, God, he was teasing... 'I mean, shouldn't you be working?'

'I thought I had been. But I'm just about done. I'll come back tomorrow and fix the tiles.' He gathered the brushes and paint cans. 'Now I'll leave you to get ready for your big night out—' his gaze drifted from her face, down her body '—although personally I think you look great just the way you are.' She looked down and with a gasp of embarrassment, clutched the shirt to her breasts. He just laughed and said, 'Try not to splash.'

Nash rubbed his hands over his face. He was tired. He'd been up most of the night, first looking for the cat and then getting her stitched up. And he'd spent the day doing something for Stacey. So that every time she went into her bathroom she'd remember him. Remember the way he'd kissed her.

He was tired, but restless too. He might have

teased her about the unexpected glimpse of her underwear, but it hadn't been funny. It had been profoundly disturbing. He'd never wanted a woman the way he wanted her. Wanted to give, not take.

He took a drink from the bottle of water, dumped the rest over his head in an effort to clear it, then dragged his hands through his damp hair. It didn't help much, except that he knew this wasn't some casual thing. If he'd just been feeling horny he would have taken up that student on her blatant invitation.

Okay, so he was, but this was something else. Something more. He worried about Stacey. Cared about what happened to her. He wanted to tell her that. Now. He wanted to see her now. He stood there, staring at the high wall, his balled fists jammed into his pockets in his frustration that she was going out...

The student! He'd forgotten to tell her about the student. She might be going out, but she'd still want to know that someone wanted to rent a room.

Stacey wasn't sure about the silk suit. Or the sleek hairstyle. It made her look a bit too much like her sister for comfort. Not a bit like herself.

Well, maybe that was a good thing. She was pretty sure that Lawrence wouldn't want her floating around barefoot in an Indian print she'd bought at Oxfam, with her unruly curls tied back in one of the children's bobbles.

The doorbell rang. She submitted to the agony of high heels, took one last look at herself and decided that there was no way she'd ever make the grade as a Stepford Wife.

Lawrence was standing on the doorstep, awkwardly clutching a spray of red roses. Her sister had probably told him that they would make a good impression; she might even have interrupted some high-powered meeting in Paris to order them for him. Stacey rescued him, taking them from him.

'Thank you,' he said, clearly grateful to be relieved of the embarrassment of handing them to her with some little speech, utterly oblivious to the fact that she should be the one saying thank you.

'You're a bit early, Lawrence. The babysitter hasn't arrived yet. Come in.'

'I'm sorry,' he apologised. 'I wasn't exactly sure where you lived and I don't like to be late.' He glanced at his watch. 'The reception starts at seven.'

'There's plenty of time,' she assured him. 'You haven't met my daughters, have you? Clover and Rosie.'

'Clover and Rosie?' he repeated. 'How pretty.'

'It's Primrose, actually,' Rosie said. Nash had a lot to answer for, quoting Fletcher... 'We were named after wild flowers. Mummy grows them, you know.'

'Does she?' Then, in that patronising tone that men unused to children always seemed to adopt, he said, 'It's a good job you weren't boys. What would she have done then?'

'If we'd been boys,' Clover said, with a dead-pan expression that boded nothing but trouble, 'Mummy would have called us Lousewort and Frogbit.'

Stacey glared at the girls, silently warning them to behave, then smiled at Lawrence. 'Come through to the kitchen and tell me what's happening tonight, while I put these in water,' she said, hoping her daughters had washed up and put everything away as they'd promised. But even if they hadn't she could scarcely leave the poor man to the tender mercies of her children. They hadn't forgiven her for going out and depriving them of Nash's company, and they were clearly in no mood to take prisoners.

She filled a vase and tried to make the stiff, long-stemmed roses look as if they were remotely organic. It was a lost cause. They were so forced that they didn't know how to bend, but she did her best and then arranged her face into a smile as she turned and said, 'It was a lovely thought, Lawrence...' The words died on her lips as she saw Nash standing in the doorway.

His hair and shirt were wet, his shorts were filthy and his boots were spattered with yellow paint. The contrast with Lawrence's dark suit, immaculate shirt and neatly knotted silk tie couldn't have been more pronounced.

The only thing the two men had in common was their expression. Total astonishment, swiftly followed by thorough disapproval.

'Nash,' she said, quickly. 'Have you come to check on the cat? She seems to be doing really well, don't you think?' He didn't say anything. 'And the kittens are thriving.'

He dragged his gaze from Lawrence to look at her, the roses she was holding. 'Nice flowers,' he said. 'Nice' as in expensive, dull, predictable, Stacey thought. Two minds with but a single thought. 'And you've had your hair done. I didn't notice earlier. I guess I was distracted.'

Her cheeks fired up as she recalled just how he'd been distracted. 'Stacey?' Lawrence touched her elbow, clearly not sure what to make of this scene but perhaps wanting to reassure her. It didn't help but, short of shaking him off, she didn't know what to do.

'What do you want, Nash?'

He held out a piece of paper. 'Nothing. I came to give you this. Someone called this morning when you were out. About a room to let?' he said, with an edge to his voice that could have cut sheet metal. When she made no move to take the message, he crossed to her, took her hand and placed the paper on her palm before wrapping her fingers shut around it. He smelt of damp earth and crushed grass and paint and she almost swooned with longing to press herself against him and have him kiss her, hold her, make the world go away. 'She left her name and telephone number.'

'Nash...' It was getting worse and worse, but what could she say? 'I was looking for someone long-term. You said you were just passing through.'

'No need to explain, Stacey. It was my mistake.' He glanced briefly at Lawrence. 'I can see exactly how things are.' His right hand was still wrapped around her fingers, but with his left he extracted a key from his pocket and placed it on the table beside her. 'Here's your key.'

'No…'

'I won't be available for cat-sitting tomorrow, Stacey.' And with that he released her, turned and walked out.

'Nash!' She started to follow him, too late pulling away from Lawrence, not caring what he thought, in her need to explain. About the room. About Lawrence. 'Nash, damn you!' He did not look back. 'I'm the one who's cat-sitting,' she shouted after him. 'She belongs on your side of the wall!'

He stopped, half-turned, almost as if he might come back. But he didn't. He just looked over his shoulder, saw Vera coming around the side of the house clutching a video and a jumbo pack of snacks. 'Rolling stones gather no cats,' he said. 'If you can't cope, take her to the animal shelter.'

'I wouldn't do that!' Stacey was angry, really angry, but Vera was staring open-mouthed and Lawrence was staring at his watch, clearly wishing he was somewhere else, so she had no choice but let it go. For now. She'd see him later. And he'd listen. She'd make him listen. Right now, she had a date with Mr Embarrassed. 'Shall we go, Lawrence?'

He opened the car door for her—a Mercedes, no less. She knew she should be impressed, but she wasn't. She didn't give a damn.

She'd rather walk with Nash than ride in this kind of luxury with Lawrence, who smelt of nothing but expensive aftershave lotion.

She wanted fresh air and loose clothes; what she'd got was heavy cologne, a close-fitting skirt and tights that were making her feel hot and uncomfortable. And she was thoroughly miserable because Nash clearly thought she was on a hot date with Lawrence. Which might have been on her sister's agenda, but certainly didn't figure on her life plan.

She couldn't do much about any of it for now, so she just fanned herself with her hand.

Lawrence cleared his throat. 'It is still very warm, isn't it? We could do with some rain to clear the air.' Oh, God. The weather. The last conversational gambit of the Englishman *in extremis*. Well, he wasn't going to ask her who Nash was, was he? Or what he was doing walking into her house without so much as a by your leave? Or why he was entrusted with her key? He was far too polite. 'I don't suppose you happened to catch the weather forecast?' he enquired.

'No. I missed it.' Gosh, darn it. She must remember to pay close attention to the weather forecast on Saturday. It would give them something to talk about over dinner. 'Would you mind if I opened the window?'

'No need.' He reached for a switch. The temperature dropped like a stone. 'Air conditioning,' he said. Yes, well, she'd worked that out for herself. About to explain that she would have preferred an open window, she was forestalled with, 'I know how you ladies hate to mess up your hair.'

He knew nothing.

Her hair demanded messing up. She wanted messed-up hair, a face free of make-up. She wanted to kick off her shoes and the waist-trimming hell of her seven denier tights and lie down in thick, cool grass.

But not with Lawrence Fordham.

CHAPTER NINE

NASH retreated to the bottom of Stacey's garden but, shaking too much to climb the wall, he was forced to stay there and confront his feelings. Well, there was a lot to confront. No doubt about them now.

This was jealousy. The genuine article. If he hadn't turned around and walked straight out of her kitchen, he'd have hit that stuffed shirt's expensive dentistry right down his throat the moment he'd touched Stacey's arm. Then, while he'd been in the mood to speak his mind, he'd have told her that she didn't need a load of make-up, or a touch-me-not hairdo, or silk clothes to look beautiful.

She'd looked wonderful with her hair tied back in a silly bobble that belonged to Rosie, absolutely fabulous in a tank top and baggy shorts, with forget-me-not-blue paint on her fingers and thighs...

Not that she'd want to know what he thought.

Considering the effort Stacey had made with her appearance, she must be making a big play for the stuffed shirt. And why shouldn't she? He might be at least ten years older than her, but there was no doubt that he had money.

And money was a big incentive. His father must have married his mother for her money, because there'd been precious little love in it.

He'd thought Stacey would have wanted more, a

lot more than that. Stuffed shirt might be able to give Rosie and Clover all those expensive extras, but he could have told her that they'd never make up for love. He was an expert on the subject.

Evidently the 'thing' at the Town Hall was not, as he had so innocently assumed—as she had so obviously meant him to assume—some local meeting about town-twinning. It clearly involved visiting dignitaries, vast swathes of mayoral chains and all the great and good of the borough. Amongst whom stuffed shirt was undoubtedly numbered.

He crashed his fist against the wall and didn't even notice the pain in his hand. The pain in his heart was already more than his brain could deal with. All his life he'd been careful to avoid this. But they said you never heard the arrow that got you.

Actually, that wasn't true. He'd known the wound was mortal in that moment when she'd looked up and he'd seen her face for the first time. Since then he'd just been kidding himself that he could handle it.

He'd go tomorrow. Take a room at a hotel in town, give his lecture and say goodbye to Archie, leave him to build his industrial units, or do whatever else he wanted with the land. Stacey wouldn't care and neither did he, not now she had other plans.

His only plans involved leaving the country at the earliest opportunity.

Actually, Stacey decided, the evening wasn't as deadly as she'd feared. Lawrence didn't seem to find networking a feminine version of himself from

Brussels, equally enthusiastic about dairy products, that much of a hardship, and she was able to renew her acquaintance, over the finger buffet, with her bank manager.

On neutral ground he was much less daunting— positively encouraging about her chances, in fact. He even introduced her to the editor of the *Maybridge Gazette*, who remembered the wild flower meadow she'd made for the school. He gave her his card and told her to get in touch once she was in business so that they could do a feature.

Maybe Dee had a point; it had been a useful evening. By the time Lawrence announced it was time to leave, though, her disturbed night was catching up with her.

'Are you sure you want to rush off?' she said, smothering a yawn, determined that her sister should have no reason for complaint. No one else seemed in any hurry to go and he'd been so deep in conversation with the Belgian lady yoghurt enthusiast that she'd been sure she'd have to tear him away. 'My babysitter will be fine for another hour. Half an hour, anyway,' she amended, quickly.

A whole hour would probably have her dozing off in the corner. And that wouldn't impress the bank manager. Although she might get her picture in the morning edition of the *Gazette*, along with an invitation for readers to send in witty captions to illustrate just how boring Town Hall receptions could be. Not at all the kind of publicity she was looking for.

'No, Stacey. I'm deeply grateful to you. I'm sure

Dee told you how much I was dreading coming along by myself. But I've taken up enough of your time for one evening.'

She blinked. That almost sounded like a brush-off. The suit hadn't cut the mustard, evidently.

Not that she was complaining. She'd done her duty, kept her promise to Dee, even made some useful contacts for the future; but right now she couldn't wait to set her toes free and fall into bed for ten solid hours of sleep.

She also needed to make her peace with Nash, but sleep was a priority. She was going to need a clear head for that one.

Nash lay outside his tent on top of the sleeping bag. It was too hot and stuffy inside. Even out in the open it was oppressive and he didn't need the weather man to tell him that the fine spell they'd been enjoying was about to end. Definitely time to be moving on.

He heard a car draw up outside Stacey's house. Then, after a moment, he heard it pull away again. He'd been holding his breath, he realised, wondering if she'd invite him in. If she'd offer stuffed shirt a piece of fruit pie just to prove that she was good 'wife' material.

But there hadn't been time for more than a quick goodnight kiss.

Even a quick kiss was more than he could bear to contemplate.

Ten minutes later Stacey's bedroom light went on. Then the bathroom light. Then everything went dark. She was home. Safe. In bed alone. He closed his eyes.

Suppose he put all his cards on the table, he thought. Explained the situation. Offered her the garden... Asked her to wait...

A gust of wind woke him. The tent flap had worked loose and was whipping back and forth noisily, and as he dragged the sleeping bag inside, great heavy drops of rain began to fall.

Stacey woke with a heart-pounding start, sitting up in bed even before she was properly awake. There had been a livid flash...

A crack of thunder directly overhead reassured her that it was nothing worse than a summer storm. Although that was bad enough. Her curtains were already flapping wetly and as she leapt out of bed to slam down the window, she discovered the carpet was soaked.

Rain streamed down the glass and she pressed her face against it, trying to see out, wondering what kind of damage the deluge would wreak on her poor, defenceless house.

Lightning lit up the sky once more, bleaching her garden, reflecting off the water lying on the grass as the rain fell faster than it could soak into the ground.

A few seconds later the thunder cracked again and she thought about Nash, wondered if he was all right. Stupid question. Unless he'd had the tent storm-rigged, he'd be soaked, along with everything he possessed. And it had been so hot he'd have had the flaps tied back to get any breath of air.

He might, or might not, be talking to her, but she still couldn't leave him out in this.

She pulled on her jogging pants and looked in on Rosie and Clover. Rosie was fast asleep but Clover stirred. 'What's that noise, Mummy?'

'Just a bit of thunder, darling. Nothing to worry about. But it's raining very heavily so I'm going to see if Nash wants to come in.' If they hadn't had that stupid row, he'd have been rattling stones up at her window long before now. 'Will you be all right?'

'No problem.' The lightning didn't penetrate through the heavy curtaining at their windows. And, despite the continuing rumble of thunder, Clover closed her eyes and went back to sleep.

Stacey didn't bother with a coat, just unhooked the heavy-duty torch from behind the door.

The rain was pouring over the guttering in an ominous way, but she didn't have time to worry about that. Instead she ran down the garden, gasping as the wind and rain buffeted at her. She was soaked through to the skin long before she reached the wall, her new hairdo plastered against her face and neck. She hadn't realised it was possible to get so wet outside of a shower.

'Nash!' She started calling him from halfway down the garden. 'Nash!' There was no response, but it was doubtful if he would hear her over the sound of the rain; the thick gurgle of water was struggling through drains not built for this kind of downpour, spilling over her inadequate guttering.

She hooked the torch over her arm and jumped

for the wall. Her fingers, cold and wet, slipped against it, but she dug in and hauled herself up. Then she unhooked the torch and shone it in the direction of his camp. There was no sign of the tent.

'Nash!' she cried, at the top of her lungs, but the sound was snatched away. Surely he must see her? Or at least the torch. He couldn't be sleeping through this?

She waved the torch madly, clutching at the wall as the wind buffeted her. For a moment she thought it shifted beneath her and glanced down. Nothing. Then, as the lightning flashed again, the wall seemed to bulge, and before she could quite register what was happening it began to fall apart.

'Idiot.' She was in an ambulance, speeding towards the A&E Department at the local hospital. 'What the devil did you think you were doing, eh?'

Nash was muddy. There was brick dust on his face, his hands were smeared with blood, but he was stroking her forehead, so that was all right.

'It was raining,' she said. 'I thought you'd get pneumonia or something.'

'You'd care?'

'Of course I'd care.' Then, because that sounded a bit too much like a declaration, she said, 'You promised to tile my bathroom tomorrow. Or do I mean today?'

She suddenly panicked, tried to move, but the paramedic stopped her. 'Better lie still, Mrs O'Neill. Until we know what's broken.'

Broken? Momentarily distracted, it took her a moment to remember why she'd tried to move. 'Who's looking after Rosie and Clover?'

'Vera. She was watching the storm from her bedroom window. She saw you go down with the wall and had the good sense to call an ambulance before she came down to help pull you out of the rubble.'

'Did she? I'll be baking her pies for the next ten years.'

'You won't be doing anything for a week or two. I don't need an X-ray to diagnose a broken ankle.'

She groaned. 'Dee'll never forgive me! I'm supposed to be going to some dinner dance on Saturday with Lawrence. She loaned me her Armani dress—'

'Shh,' he said. 'Don't worry about it.' Oh, God, he probably thinks I'm raving, Stacey decided.

'No, honestly—'

Nash squeezed her hand. He'd been holding it all the time, she realised, and it gave her a warm, fuzzy feeling. Or maybe that was the painkiller. Anyway, she was glad she'd realised, so that she could enjoy it. 'I'm sure he'll understand. Do you, er, want me to phone him?'

'Lawrence? Good Lord, no—'

Nash felt an ungallant surge of pleasure that she didn't want the stuffed shirt guy to see her covered with mud and blood and bruises. 'What about your sister? Will she be back home?'

'I don't know. But there's no point in phoning her in the middle of the night. She'll only want to tell me off for messing up her plans.'

Her plans? 'She won't. If she's going to shout at anyone, it'll be me.'

'Then you're definitely not to phone her. I don't want her to have that much fun—' She started to laugh, then winced. 'Are you sure it's just my ankle?'

'You got off lightly. This could have been a lot worse.'

And he would never have forgiven himself, Nash knew. Never have been able to live with himself. The ambulance came to a halt and the doors were flung open.

'Will I have to stay here, Nash?' she asked, clinging to his hand as the stretcher was lifted out. 'Someone will have to look after Clover and Rosie. And the kittens—'

'I will,' he called after her. I will, he repeated silently to himself. Trust me. And then she was wheeled into a cubicle to be assessed, while he was sidetracked to provide her name and such details as he knew about her to the receptionist.

It seemed like hours before he saw her again. 'Simple broken ankle. Apart from that it's just cuts and bruises,' the nurse said. 'But you're going to be very sore for a few days, Mrs O'Neill. We're trying to find a bed for you now. We're a bit crowded.'

'I don't want a bed, I want to go home.'

'Have you got someone to take care of you at home?'

'I'll manage,' she said.

The nurse looked doubtful, glanced at him for some kind of confirmation. Well, that wasn't a problem. If it hadn't been for him the accident would never have happened. 'There's no need to worry,

Nurse. I'll be staying with her until she's on her feet again.'

'But—'

He cut off Stacey's protestations. 'You were coming to offer me the spare room when the wall collapsed, weren't you? I certainly hope so, because my tent blew away in the storm.'

'Did you lose everything?'

'No. I'd moved most of my stuff into the office before it started to blow really hard.'

'You mean I needn't have bothered!' He didn't think it would be wise to comment. 'And now you feel guilty and think you've got to look after me. Well, you don't. You wanted to move on—'

'And you want someone long-term,' he said, deliberately misunderstanding her. 'I could share with that student, if you like,' he offered. 'Then you'll have someone permanent when I've gone.'

Distracted she said, 'But I thought the student was a girl?'

'Hell, yes. You wouldn't expect me to share a double bed with a bloke, would you?' The porter arrived to wheel her away. 'What do you say?'

'Idiot?' she offered.

'I'll take that as a yes, then.' He glanced at the nurse. 'Is it okay to take her home? Where can I organise some transport?'

'I'll show you.' She led the way from the cubicle, giving him an old-fashioned look. He shrugged. 'Look, I was kidding about the student, okay?'

The nurse was not impressed. 'You mean it

wouldn't do to let Mrs O'Neill know that you're in love with her?'

In love? As in till-death-us-do-part, in love?

Nash had a flash of what it must have been like to be Stacey on top of the wall in that brief instant before it crumbled beneath her.

A this-can't-be-happening-to-me moment.

But it had.

This was all wrong, Stacey thought. Lying in bed in the morning while everyone else rushed around. Not that it was exactly peaceful.

'Mummy, where are my shorts? It's PE today.'

'In the ironing basket.'

'You mean they're not ironed!' She raced out of the bedroom and thumped down the stairs. 'Nash! They need ironing. Can you iron?'

'Rosie, you can manage!' she shouted after her daughter. 'Nash, you do not have to iron Rosie's shorts!'

She heard the telltale squeak of the ironing board and groaned. Then she heard her sister's voice and tried very hard to burrow under the bedclothes as her feet pounded up the stairs.

It didn't work. 'What on earth is going on here? That man says you've broken your ankle. Do you know he's in your kitchen ironing the girls' shorts—'

'He didn't have to. They could have managed.'

Dee sat on the edge of the bed and Stacey winced. 'What happened?'

*   *   *

'I had a bit of a fall on Monday night.'

'Monday? This happened on Monday? I stay away a couple of nights and everything falls apart.'

'Not everything. Just the wall. And it's nothing, really.'

'I saw the wall, Stacey. It was scarcely nothing.'

'I'll be fine in a day a two.'

'You don't look as if you'll be fine. You've got a black eye—'

'Thanks, Dee. I really wanted to know that.' She'd slept most of Tuesday and hadn't been near a mirror yet. Now she didn't want to.

'Shouldn't you be in hospital?'

'They didn't have a bed. It was a trolley in the corridor or Nash bringing me home.'

'But that's disgraceful!'

'No. Really. It was fine. He didn't have to bring me on the back of his motorbike. They gave us a lift in an ambulance—'

Dee was not amused. 'For heaven's sake, you should have called Tim. Look, we'll get you moved over to my house straight away. Ingrid can look after you and the girls while I'm at work—'

'No, Dee.'

'Be reasonable—'

'I'm not going anywhere. I'm fine. Nash is doing a great job. He's going to help me downstairs today, once the girls are at school. I'll have some breakfast, sit in the garden.'

'And what'll he be doing?'

'His name is Nash, Dee. Nash Gallagher. And he'll be tiling my bathroom.' She eased herself up a little and wondered if it was possible that all she'd broken was her ankle. Her body felt as if it had been pulverised. 'You'll find your car keys on the dresser.'

Dee stood up. 'I'll come back later, then. If you're sure you're all right.' She didn't go. 'Can I bring you anything?'

'Grapes would be lovely.' She mentally urged her sister through the door.

'Nothing else?'

'Nothing.'

'Well, if you're sure…' Then, finally getting around to what she really wanted to know, 'Did you, er, get to the reception before the accident?'

'Yes, Dee. Lawrence brought me roses as instructed and we had a lovely time.'

'Lovely?'

She'd overdone it. 'Useful. A very useful evening. He networked like mad with a Belgian dairy—' about to say 'dairy maid', she stopped herself. Somehow she didn't think Dee would find that amusing '—dairy producer. And I networked with my bank manager. You'd have been proud of both of us. Really.'

Dee looked doubtful, but headed for the door. 'I'll see you later.' Then she opened her bag and came back. 'Here, you'd better have this.' It was her mobile phone. 'Just in case.'

She was tempted to ask in case of what, but suspected she already knew what the answer would be. 'Don't be silly, Dee. If I take that I'll be answering calls for you all morning.'

'I can redirect incoming calls.'

'Can you? How clever. It's sweet of you to offer, Dee, I know your mobile is like a second child to you, but there's no need. Nash has already given me his.' She lifted the mobile Nash had left with her the day before, so that she could call the people she was supposed to be gardening for during the next couple of weeks. It was one of those really tiny, really powerful cellphones, just like her sister's. 'Snap,' she said.

'What can I get you?'

'Out of this bed. I want to brush my teeth properly, amongst other things.'

'Okay. Put your arm around my neck.' He bent so that she could reach, then eased her carefully into a sitting position. She said a lot of short rude words as her bruises clashed and jangled with her grazes. 'Well, that was instructive.'

'Shut up and help me to my feet.'

She was still wearing the gown she'd been put into at the hospital and was aware of it flapping at the rear. 'Your bum is turning a really interesting colour.'

'I don't want to know that. And you shouldn't be looking.'

'Sorry,' he said, but not sounding it as he took her weight, easing her across to the bathroom, then lowering her gently onto the seat. He tore off a chunk of toilet paper and put it into her hand. She considered telling him that she could manage, then decided that she might just be fooling herself.

'Just shout when you're done and I'll come and help you wash.'

'You don't have to.'

'Okay, be proud. I'll come and pick you up off the floor when I've done the washing up. Or maybe you'd rather go to your sister's?'

'I'll call. I'll call.'

Actually, she didn't have any choice. She couldn't get up. But he left her sitting where she was while he filled the sink with warm water. It should have been embarrassing, but it wasn't. It was comfortable. As if she'd known him for ever. Then he took a washcloth and gently washed her face and neck, easing the hospital gown over her shoulders to wash her back and arms as she clutched the papery throwaway garment against her breasts.

'This is like being a child,' she said, as he offered her the soaped cloth and she gingerly sponged her front under the covering of the gown. Then, when she was done, he lifted a clean nightdress over her head and helped her up so that she could brush her teeth.

He'd remade her bed and, despite her brave statements about getting up and sitting in the garden, she was glad to get back to it. When she was settled, propped up with a load of pillows, Nash brushed out her hair, which had reverted to unruly curls. 'Do you want me to tie it back for you?'

'Please. You'll find something on the dressing table.'

Among the clutter of hairbands and plant ties and seed catalogues, he found a photograph of a good-looking man in a rugby shirt laughing at something the girl behind the camera was saying, or doing. 'Is this your husband?' He held up the snapshot so that she could see from the bed.

'Yes, that's Mike.'

'You must miss him.' There was a long moment of silence. 'I'm sorry. You probably don't want to talk about him.'

'No. It's all right. Really. It's just tough on Clover and Rosie,' she said, 'not having a daddy. I know that a lot of children live with one parent, these days, but they don't even have the consolation of someone else to go to, someone to spoil them and compete for their love.'

'Believe me, it's overrated.'

'Your parents split up?'

'Oh, no. They weren't that civilised. They stayed together in order to make one another as miserable as possible. But they indulged in the spoiling game when they were point-scoring.'

'I'm so sorry, Nash.'

'It's okay. I was lucky. I had a grandfather to go to when things got really bad.' He put the photograph back and picked up a handful of hair-ties. 'Now then, ma'am,' he said, holding them up for her inspection. 'Do you want the duck, the daisies or the roses?'

'The daisies, please.'

'And for breakfast?'

'I can't remember the last time I had breakfast in bed.'

'Better make the most of it, then. A lightly boiled egg with toast soldiers?'

She laughed, then pulled a face as all her aches jarred. 'Bliss,' she said, wincing. 'No, honestly,' she said, as he caught her hair back, running his fingers through it, stroking them against her scalp, lifting it from her neck.

Absolute bliss.

CHAPTER TEN

STACEY had breakfast, took the painkillers Nash gave her, then drifted off to sleep. When she woke, there was a huge basket of flowers by her bed, a florist's confection in shades of pink: roses and carnations and star-gazer lilies with their overpowering scent and tiresome pollen. She didn't need to look at the card to know who they were from.

With warmest wishes for a speedy recovery, Lawrence.

Although surely the writing on the card belonged to her sister? She must have stopped at the florist's on the way into the office. Fast worker, her sister.

'Nash!' she called. He appeared with such immediacy that she suspected he must have been sitting on the stairs, waiting for her to wake up. 'Can you please take these away? The scent is giving me a headache.'

'Won't your eager swain expect to see them beside your bed?' he asked.

God forbid, she thought, at the idea of Lawrence trying to make small talk in her bedroom. Then, as she took in the pile of specialist seed catalogues—her favourite bedtime reading—that had slithered untidily to the floor, and the offputting clutter of plant ties and labels on her dressing table, she thought maybe it wouldn't be such a bad idea to let

him see what she was really like. And it would serve
Dee right for making him come. 'If he comes to see
me—' and she just knew that her sister would make
it impossible for him to refuse '—you can bring
them back.'

'Thanks.' She caught the slightly off note in his
voice and was forced to smother the idiotic grin that
threatened to break out all over her face.

'Where do you want me to put them?'

'The dining room?' she suggested. 'It's cool in
there and they'll last longer.'

'Oh, right.' He rubbed his chin against his shoulder, leaving a streak of pale grout against the black
tank-top he was wearing. No man had the right to
look that sexy, that desirable. It wasn't fair on a
woman who was determined to be sensible, but was
finding it incredibly hard.

'What?' he said.

She started to shake her head, decided against it.
'Nothing. You've got grout in your hair.'

'Have I?' He lifted his hand, but let it fall before
it connected with his hair. 'You can get it later for
me.' And she knew they were both thinking about
that moment in the garden, when she'd picked the
shard of glass from his hair and they'd come within
an ace of falling into each other's arms. Two
minutes after they'd met. Maybe she should call Dee
and tell her she'd changed her mind about staying
at her place. All this caring meant a lot of touching.

It was putting a severe strain on her life plan.

'Are you ready for something to eat, or will you
wait until I've collected the girls from school?

They're having fish fingers. Special request. But you can have something more grown-up if you like.'

The phone rang. Stacey jumped, then handed it to Nash. 'It'll be for you.'

Nash took it, pressed 'receive' and gave the number.

'Dr Gallagher?' The voice was brisk, feminine.

'Yes?'

'Dr Gallagher, this is Jennie Taylor from Botanic Survey International. We received your message about delaying your departure date. The Director wants to know if you'll be available to leave by the end of the month to set things up at your base.'

The end of the month was ten days away. He looked at Stacey. Thought about a year in South America. No contest. 'I'm sorry, I have other commitments. If you're in that big a hurry you'll have to find someone else.'

There was a moment of stunned silence. Well, that was reasonable. *He* wasn't quite sure he believed what he'd just said, either.

'I'll get back to you,' she said.

He put the phone on stand-by. She could leave a message. He returned the phone to Stacey, who was desperately trying to conceal her curiosity.

She hadn't believed in his career as a botanist, he fancied. And he hadn't exactly gone out of his way to convince her. It hadn't mattered before, but now—well, now it seemed important that she take him on face value. If she took him at all. If all she was looking for was a meal-ticket, then Lawrence was her man. But if she wanted to know who was calling him, he'd tell her. 'It was Botanic Survey International,' he said. 'They want me to lead an expedition.' Then he grinned.

'Botanic Survey International?' Stacey looked at him, trying to read his face. Mike had been easy to read. Nash wasn't much like him after all. Deeper, more complex. He was teasing her... She was sure he was teasing her. Almost. 'And you turned them down?'

'Your need is greater.'

'Oh, sure.' He was making it up. It was just someone offering him a few days' work. Could he afford to turn it down? Maybe she should be making more of an effort. 'Can you give me a hand up? I need the bathroom.'

He bent so that she could hook her arm around his neck. She must be feeling at lot better because this time she scarcely felt the muscle-grating agony of movement; she was too busy struggling with the rush of sensations as her cheek collided with his chest, as she was overwhelmed by the sharp scent of clean sweat on a man's skin. If they could bottle that, they'd have riots in the streets...

He looked down her. 'Okay?' he asked. No. Not okay. Very far from okay. But she looked up in an effort to reassure him. Smile brightly. Keep going... Except the smile wouldn't come. And he wasn't smiling either, and for a moment she thought that he was going to kiss her again. He did. He brushed his lips gently against the bruise on her forehead. 'Don't overreach yourself.'

No. She really mustn't do that. 'I can do it,' she

said, swallowing hard and making a big effort. But in the end he just picked her up and carried her across to the bathroom.

And that was when she discovered he hadn't been sitting on the stairs waiting for her to wake up. Why he had grout in his hair. She could just see him, spreading it on the wall and then dragging his fingers through that thick cowlick that flopped over his forehead…

Now the tiles were done and the effect was beautiful. 'Oh, Nash! It looks great!' He'd even hung the blind, the soft voile billowing lightly in the breeze from the garden. And there was a posy of ox-eye daisies in a jug on the shelf. She reached out, touched a petal. 'I just love these,' she said.

'Leucanthemum vulgare,' he said. Then, when she glanced up, eyes narrowed, 'I looked it up.'

'Right.' So why didn't she believe that? And why was her heart beating so hard? As if this was important, much more important than a kiss… 'You can put me down now,' she said, needing to catch her breath.

He set her carefully on her feet, still holding her, steadying her, while she got her balance. She grabbed the basin, unable to think clearly while he was holding her. Down in the garden, there were workmen clearing the mess left by the collapse of the wall.

'Where did they come from?'

'Who?' Nash looked past her. 'Oh, them. They arrived this morning, I guess the developer must have organised it. You'll be getting an offer of compensation for the accident, soon, I imagine.'

'Compensation?'

'The wall was in a dangerous state.' There was a muscle working in his jaw. 'It could have fallen any time, hurt Clover or Rosie.'

'But it didn't.' It probably wouldn't have collapsed now if she hadn't been using it as a right of way. 'The accident was my fault. I shouldn't have been climbing on the wall. I'd warned the children often enough.' She sighed. 'They'll probably put up a larchlap fence in its place. Pity.'

'You don't want to leave here, do you, Stacey?' She shook her head. 'You'd do anything to stay?'

'I am staying. I didn't think I could do it but, after Monday—well, I've made some big decisions.'

'I see.'

'Not that I'm in much of a position to do anything about them.'

'You'll soon mend. Can you manage in here?' He was the one anxious to put some distance between them now.

'Yes, thanks.' She held onto the basin and gazed longingly into the bath. 'Nash...'

'What?'

He sounded so unexpectedly sharp that she lost her nerve. Just as well, really. Asking him to help her take a bath was not in the least bit wise. Covered with bruises, she might not be any man's idea of a good time, but self-torture had never seemed a particularly bright move. 'You won't forget to take those flowers downstairs, will you?'

*   *   *

Nash opened the dining room door. He hadn't been in the room before and for a moment assumed that he'd got it wrong. There was a dining table and chairs, but when Stacey had said she'd been redecorating she'd been exaggerating.

Someone had started stripping the paper, it was true, but since it had come away from the wall with chunks of plaster adhering to it they'd given up long before it was finished. The result was a spectacular mess.

He looked at the expensive array of flowers. Surely she hadn't meant him to leave the flowers in here? Wouldn't Lawrence be mortally offended?

Actually, that seemed as good a reason to leave them there as any, so he dumped them, closed the door and went to sort out tea.

Dee Harrington was sitting in the kitchen. He paused in the doorway. 'Oh, hi. I didn't hear you arrive. Stacey's in the bathroom.'

'I didn't come to see Stacey; I came to talk to you.'

'Did you? Can I make you a cup of something?'

'Please don't bother yourself. I'm not like Stacey. I'm not taken in by all this New Man stuff.'

Nash noticed that the washing machine had stopped and was sorely tempted to empty it and start pegging out the sheets. But he restrained himself, pulled out a chair and joined her at the kitchen table. 'Do you want to tell me what's bothering you?'

'You, Mr Gallagher. You're bothering me. Stacey's had her heart broken once and I don't want her going through that again.'

'And what makes you think I'll break her heart.'

'It's inevitable. You're a clone of Mike. Her husband,' she added, in case he didn't know. 'He looked just like you. Fair hair, blue eyes and muscles.'

'It's not something I can do much about, Ms Harrington. It's just a simple combination of genetics and hard work.'

'Mike worked hard, too. And played hard. He never stopped playing. Rugby, basketball—when he should have been home playing at being a husband. And he liked grown-up toys, too. Motorcycles were his favourite. Closely followed by real live dolls... Stacey was a good loyal wife, who stuck by him and cried a lot when he died. She deserves something better this time.'

'And you plan to make sure she gets it?'

'Wouldn't you? If she was your sister?' She leaned forward. 'Lawrence Fordham is a good man and he can give her a good life, but she won't look at him while you're around. She needs to move on, Mr Gallagher. You're just a step backwards for her.'

'I think maybe you're underestimating your sister, Ms Harrington. And I know you're underestimating me. Now, if you'll excuse me,' he said, rising to his feet, 'I've got to get Stacey settled before I fetch the girls from school. Shall I tell her you called? Or would you prefer it if I kept this little chat between ourselves?'

She stood up, her face flushed with anger. 'You are so sure of yourself! You've found a nice little comfort zone, a needy widow with her own home, and you've a real knack for making yourself indispensable. Well, be warned, Mr Gallagher, Stacey might be a push-over, but I am not. If you've got anything to hide, you'd better make some excuse and leave now—because I'll be checking up on you.'

'You'll stay here and look after her, will you?' It was a challenge. 'Or maybe Mr Fordham will roll up his sleeves and get the dusting done—'

'Just go and I'll take her home with me,' she hissed. 'There are plenty of people to look after her there.'

'I don't think so. As you say, I've got everything I ever wanted here.' He grabbed a kitten that was making a break for it across the kitchen floor and returned him to his mother.

'Nash!' Stacey's voice drifted down from the top of the stairs. 'I'm ready to come downstairs now.'

'Then I'd better come and make sure you're decent. You've got a visitor.' He smiled at Dee. 'You can see how it is. A New Man's work is never done.'

'Lawrence… You didn't have to come out of your way.' Not that she believed he'd had much choice. 'You already sent flowers. I have them upstairs,' she added quickly, in case he wondered where they were. Where *were* they? She remembered asking Nash to take them away… 'Do sit down.'

Stacey was draped, like some expiring nineteenth-century heroine, over the sofa. The sofa somewhat spoiled the illusion, being of the ancient, squashy

variety. And the children didn't help, either, since
they insisted on staying to watch cartoons on the
television.

They clearly made Lawrence nervous.

'Where's Nash?' she asked them. Normally they
trailed after him like a shadow.

'He's fixing something,' Clover said. 'He said if
we stayed out of the garden for half an hour he'd
give us some dribbling practice before bedtime.'
And she turned the volume up.

Oh, well. It was probably best to let Lawrence see
them all at their worst... He was perched on the
edge of an armchair, clearly way out of his depth.
'Thank you for the flowers. They were lovely.'

'Oh, were they? Well, Dee organised them—she's
so good at that sort of thing. Um, how are you,
Stacey? I knew you'd taken a fall, but I didn't realise...'

How bad she'd look? 'It looks worse than it is.
Really. But I'm sorry to have messed up Saturday
night.'

'It's not a problem.' It wasn't? 'When Dee told
me what had happened, I phoned Cecile straight
away and she was delighted to come in your place.'

He looked positively animated, for Lawrence, and
she got the distinct impression that Cecile was not
the only one delighted at the turn events had taken.
She managed to bear the pain of being supplanted
in his affections with a reasonable degree of equa-
nimity.

'Cecile?' she enquired.

'Mlle Latour. You met her on Monday night. At

the reception,' he prompted when she still looked blank.

'Did I?' Did he mean the Belgian dairy queen? She rather thought he did. Well, well, well. 'Yes, I remember.'

'She's coming over on the Eurostar on Saturday morning.'

'All the way from Brussels? For dinner?'

'Well, no. For the weekend.' She noticed the slightest tinge of pink colouring his dairy-pale cheeks and the penny finally dropped. That was why he had been in such a hurry to ditch her on Monday night. He'd lined up a late supper with his Gallic counterpart. And without permission from Dee. Sly old Lawrence. They'd both underestimated him. 'I'm delighted for you. Honestly.' Then, 'Have you told Dee, yet?' He looked slightly panic-stricken at the thought, but Stacey patted his hand. 'Be brave. She can't kill you.' She'd undoubtedly reserve that fate for a sister who was too slow-witted to make the most of her chances.

Nash had two choices. Sit and glower at Lawrence Fordham, or get on with something that would do Stacey a lot more good than a bunch of hothouse flowers.

He reckoned he might have a week before Dee Harrington found out exactly who he was. It didn't give him a lot of time, but he was determined that Stacey make her mind up between him and Lawrence before then.

Meantime he'd sent his little chaperons inside so

that he could concentrate on fixing the loose tiles. He didn't want to be distracted with worries about what Fordham was up to while he was on the roof.

'Stacey, I have to go out tomorrow morning.' He'd seen her into bed, tucked her in and now seemed reluctant to leave. Well, that was fine by her. 'Will you be all right, or do you want me to ask Vera to come round and sit with you? Or your sister?'

'Good grief, spare me that.'

'Vera, then. I'd be happier if there was someone here with you.'

'I'm feeling a lot better, Nash. And I've got my sticks if I need to hop to the bathroom.' She'd been practising during the afternoon.

'I'll leave the phone for you.'

'Thanks. I suppose I'll have to get one of my own if I'm going into business. I'll be able to walk along the street talking into it and looking important.'

'Are you? Going into business?'

'You said it. Reach for the moon. Unfortunately, before I can do that, the bank manager insists I have a business plan. And Archie says I need more land.'

'Archie?'

'Archie Baldwin. The old chap that used to run the garden centre. I went to see him. I thought maybe he knew what was going on.' She decided to push him a little. 'I mean, you might have been clearing the place up, but not for any developer.' He didn't comment. 'I thought if the garden centre was going to be regenerated, I might be able to negotiate an outlet.'

'Part of the business plan?'

'Mmm.'

'And what did Archie tell you?'

'Nothing. I always thought he owned the place, but I guess he must just have been renting it. He suggested I ask you.'

'So why haven't you?'

Why hadn't she? She wasn't sure, so she grinned. 'Oh, you know, Monday was all rush, rush, rush. Then you were in such a bad mood when you called round with that phone number.' She shrugged. 'And since then I've been lying on my bed of pain.' Or perhaps, she thought, she was just making excuses. Perhaps she wasn't sure she'd like the answer.

An out-of-control libido was not the best judge of character, as she knew to her cost. She was desperately afraid she might have got it wrong again.

'I'm sorry.' He crossed to her, knelt at the side of the bed, took her hand between both of his. He looked so solemn that she was seriously disturbed.

'Sorry?'

'I should have told you. I don't know why I didn't.'

'Told me what? Nash, please—'

'You're right, I'm not clearing the place up for a developer. Archie's my grandfather.'

'Archie?' To say that she was stunned would have been an understatement of monumental proportions. That she didn't doubt it was even more surprising. But there was a likeness...not so much facial, but physical. The economy of movement, the deftness of touch. The total control over their environment...

'But why didn't he say?' She was deeply hurt. She'd thought Archie was her friend. She'd thought Nash was, too. 'Why didn't you?'

He lifted her hand to his forehead, as if somehow she might be able to understand if she could feel what he was feeling. 'I used to spend all my time in that garden when I was a child. I felt safe there.' He was quiet for a moment. 'Then, about twenty years ago, there was a huge family row. Archie accused my mother of neglecting me...well, everyone said a lot of things that are better forgotten. I was thirteen years old and the only one in the family everyone was talking to. And I refused to be my mother's messenger, or my father's. It was easier not to talk to any of them.'

'Oh, Nash, but that's awful. Dee's a pain sometimes but I know she loves me and I love her.'

'Then Archie was sick and I knew I had to make my peace with him. He hasn't changed much. He's still a stubborn old mule, but he asked me to look in at the garden. Say goodbye for him. He was carried out on a stretcher, you see.'

'I know. I found him.'

'Then you saved his life.' He kissed her fingers, looked up at her. 'Thank you for that. I'd never have forgiven myself...'

'It's all right,' she whispered. 'It's all right.'

'When I saw the state of the place...' He broke off as if it was too much for him to explain. 'I thought I'd just weed around the peach trees. He always lifted me up to pick the first one.'

'Did he?' She had a sweet image of a cream-haired boy biting into the ripe fruit. *Have you ever tasted a peach ripe from the tree?* He'd kissed her and thought of his warmest childhood memory. There was something so heart-rendingly sweet about that.

'After that...' He seemed to falter.

'You just kept going?'

'No. After that you climbed over the wall and I couldn't tear myself away.' Nash knew that was below the belt. Unfair. Lawrence Fordham didn't have the heart-beating quiet of the night alone with her. But all was fair in love... And Nash was, without doubt, in love with this woman. What he'd said was no more than the truth. 'Stacey—'

'Shh. Come here...' She moved over to give him some room to join her on the bed. His mouth dried. He wanted this, wanted her heaven alone knew how much, but he wanted it too much to make a mistake.

'You're sure?'

'I just want to hold you, Nash.'

Right. He'd probably die from sensory overload, but he undoubtedly deserved it, so he kicked off his boots, swung himself onto the bed beside her and put his arm around her. She was warm and sweet and he wanted to wrap her up in his arms and make the kind of sweet, giving love the poets wrote about. But if she just wanted to hold him, that would be good.

'Excuse me...' Oh, Lord. Major error. Total misunderstanding. 'Don't you take your socks off before you get into bed?'

Into bed? Not just on top of the bed? He had a

sudden tantalising glimpse of paradise. 'I usually take off everything.'

'Then I suggest you do that.' Her eyes were a soft invitation. 'And while you're on your feet, you can turn out the light. The way I look at the moment, I think I'd prefer it if we did this by touch.'

CHAPTER ELEVEN

'MUMMY, it's late.'

'Late?' Stacey opened her eyes and blinked against the sun shining through the window. Clover was peering into her face. 'How late?' She glanced at the bedside table, which looked all wrong. 'Where's the clock?'

'Over there.' She trotted round the bed, said, 'Hi, Nash.' And brought it back. 'It's a quarter past eight,' she said. 'Look.'

Stacey looked. Clover was right… Then her brain caught up. Nash. She sat up, not even noticing the aches. He'd rolled over and was peering up at her from the warm nest of the bedclothes. Oh, damn!

'Mummy…' What on earth was she going to say? How was she going to explain this to her knowing little girl? 'If Nash is going to sleep in here with you, can I have the spare room? I'm too big to share with Rosie now.'

It was that simple? 'We'll talk about it. Later. Go and get washed and make sure Rosie is up—' Nash was grinning. 'It's not funny,' she hissed.

He kissed her bruised thigh and then looked up at her. 'No. It's deadly serious. I'm deadly serious— you know that, don't you?'

She didn't. She didn't know anything. Except they were late and Clover would probably be entertaining the entire class with her expectations of a baby brother. 'Help me up,' she said. 'It's going to need both of us to get the girls to school on time.'

'I can handle it.' He rolled out of bed, tugged on the shorts he'd discarded the night before and then, when he reached the door, he looked back and grinned. 'Stay there. Don't move a muscle. I'm coming right back.'

And he did, with a cup of tea, a slice of toast and a quick kiss before he walked Clover and Rosie across the village to school. And she bet that had been causing all kinds of gossip, too. Even before there were grounds for any.

Oh, well, gather ye Rosebay Willow Herbs while ye may... She eased herself out of bed, and with the help of crutches supplied by the hospital, she made it to the bathroom. Not as much fun as being carried, but a girl had to make an effort.

She'd washed herself and brushed her teeth by the time he returned. He was impressed, but not impressed enough to stay and undo all her good work.

'I saw Vera when I walked the girls across to school,' he said, reaching for the razor. 'She's coming round to sit with you.'

'There's no need. I can get about now.'

He looked doubtfully at the crutches. 'You might fall. And I'm not sure how long I'm going to be.'

'I thought you said you were just going to be out this morning.'

'More like until after lunch,' he said, covering his chin with shaving foam. 'I want to go and see Archie, too.'

'Give him my love.' He stroked the razor up his throat and she watched him for a moment. It had been a long time since she'd watched a man shave and she'd always thought it was the sexiest thing... So intimate, so dangerous. One slip... A lot like love. 'Nash.' He turned. 'Thank you. For last night.'

'It was my pleasure.' He smiled and leaned nearer to drop a kiss on her forehead, leaving a smear of foam. He wiped it away with the pad of his thumb. 'Tonight we'll try it again, with the light on.'

'But Clover and Rosie—'

'Clover and Rosie are not a problem.' No, Clover and Rosie would be over the moon... 'But you might give some thought about how you're going to break the news that I'm staying to your sister.'

'You're staying?'

He paused in his attentions to his chin and looked at her through the mirror. 'Don't you want me to?'

'Yes,' she said. This wasn't the moment for pretence, games. If they couldn't be honest with one another, they might as well stop right now, before it got beyond stopping without a lot of heartache. A lot of pain. Actually, the thought of him leaving was already so painful that it had probably gone too far for that. 'I want you to stay very much. But you said you were a rolling stone.'

'Yeah, well maybe I just hit an obstacle and fell into a ditch.'

'Oh, right!'

He swished his razor in the water and grinned. 'A delightful ditch.'

She tried to keep a straight face, but it was impossible. She wanted to smile for England. 'Poor Dee, she's having a bad week.' She turned on her crutches and headed for the door, then, suddenly feeling bold. 'Nash—'

'Mmm?'

'Could you help me take a bath this evening?'

He stopped shaving, apparently having a little trouble with the grip on his razor. 'You really know how to make a man want to rush home, don't you?'

Stacey wondered if Nash had reconsidered the job he'd been offered the day before. Assuming it wasn't to lead an expedition up the Amazon. But it couldn't be that, because when he left the house he was wearing nothing more formal than clean jeans and a plain dark green T-shirt under his leathers.

He kissed her and held her for a moment before he left, felt her involuntary shiver beneath the track-suit he'd helped her into. 'What is it?'

'Nothing.' He continued to look at her. 'I just don't like motorbikes.'

'No?' He pulled on his helmet. 'Well, maybe it is time to trade it in for something sensible. Something for four.'

'A Volvo?' She was forcing a laugh, but never had a Volvo seemed so desirable. 'They're safe. Maybe you could get a yellow one...I read somewhere that people who drive yellow cars have fewer accidents...'

'That sounds...interesting.'

'No. Look. I'm sorry. I'm being stupid. You don't have to change for me. Not a thing. Honestly.'

'Just meeting you changed me, Stacey. Loving you... There aren't words to describe what that has done.'

Loving you.

Easy to say. Hard to live.

She diverted herself by wondering what he really did when he wasn't clearing up Archie's garden. And then, as she limped slowly around the house and saw what he had done for her, not just the bathroom, but repainting the kitchen door too—fixing the handle, she knew. She touched the shelf. It had been put up at a slight angle. Not enough to really make a fuss about. Just enough to irritate the eye. Now it didn't.

That was what Nash did. He lived what he was. She'd been wrong about him. He wasn't a bit like Mike. He might have the same build, the same colouring, but that meant nothing. Mike had been a beautiful hunk of a man, but it had all been on the surface.

Nash wasn't like that. He wasn't just beautiful to look at, he was beautiful inside, too. He didn't wait to be asked, he just saw what needed to be done and did it. The way he'd fixed her lawn mower. The way he'd just gone ahead and decorated her bathroom. The way he'd made love to her, slow and gentle. Giving not taking.

He might not have the kind of financial back-up of Lawrence Fordham, but if he said he loved her she could believe him. He'd love her and he'd love her children and care for them with everything he had. And that was all anyone could ask of a man.

'Stacey?' Vera stuck her head around the back door. 'You're up and about. That's great!' Then she looked doubtful.

'What?'

She giggled. 'It just occurred to me that if I was getting the kind of nursing you're getting, I'd be inclined to malinger a little.' Stacey's face flamed and she laughed out loud. 'Okay. I get the picture. It's too new to talk about. Where's the coffee?'

They were on their second cup when Dee arrived, waving the *Maybridge Gazette*. 'Why didn't you tell me?' She seemed torn between anger and laughter. Not a good combination.

Stacey sighed and put down her cup. 'Tell you what, Dee?'

'About Nash Gallagher, of course!'

Dear Lord, it wasn't in the morning paper, was it? She glanced at Vera, wondering if she was a stringer for the *Gazette*'s gossip page. It didn't usually amount to more than local engagements and the more colourful divorces. One night of passion, very gentle passion at that, as a concession to her ankle and comprehensive array of bruises, didn't quite seem to fit the bill.

Vera looked blank, but Dee didn't leave them in suspense for long. 'Look, it's on the front page.' And she slammed it down on the table in front of them. BALDWIN HEIR TO LECTURE AT UNIVERSITY. 'Nash Gallagher is Archer Baldwin's grandson, for heaven's sake.' Archer?

Did she mean Archie? Stacey had always assumed it was short for Archibald, but on reflection Archibald Baldwin wouldn't be the world's greatest coupling of names. Not that she'd even known his name was Baldwin until she'd visited him at hospital. 'He's Archer Baldwin's grandson and you let me stand in your kitchen and call him a labourer!'

'What?' Stacey's mind was scrabbling to make sense of what her sister was saying. Make sense of Nash's photograph on the front page of the *Gazette*. He looked sweaty, but triumphant. As if he'd just emerged from some swamp with a newly discovered plant specimen. But then, according to the caption, he had. 'Actually,' she said, slowly, 'I think it would be more accurate to say that Nash let you call him a labourer.' She tore her gaze from the newspaper. 'I did try to stop you—not because he wasn't a labourer, but because you were being so damned rude.' Dee blushed crimson as she relived the moment. Well, Stacey thought, you saw something new every day. 'But I still don't understand. Archie isn't rich.'

'You've got to be kidding!' Dee was staring at her as if she'd come from some other planet. 'This village was just part of his estate at one time. Everyone who lived here worked on it. Mike's uncle was his gamekeeper; that's how he got the cottage.' Her face must have still looked blank, because Dee explained it in more simple terms. 'When Archer Baldwin broke up the estate he gave his workers the cottages they'd lived in all their lives. Gave them, Stacey. Not sold, not even at sitting tenant prices.

Gave.' She sat down. 'Is there any coffee left?' she asked.

Vera poured her a cup. 'Dee's right, Stacey. My mother was a cleaner up at the Hall. That's how we got our house.'

'You're too young to remember—heck I'm only just old enough to remember,' Dee said, 'but it made the national papers.'

'*What* did?'

'He disinherited his daughter, said she wasn't fit to be a Baldwin because of the way she'd treated her son. Sold up the estate, gave millions away and then dropped out of sight. Became a bit of a recluse.'

'Dee, Archie ran the garden centre on the other side of that wall. I gave him a hand when he was busy. I called the ambulance when he had a stroke…'

'Archie?' Her eyes widened. 'You mean that old man is Archer Baldwin?'

'It seems unlikely that there are two Archie Baldwins living around here,' she said, impatiently. 'Of course it's him!' She looked over Vera's shoulder at the small photograph of a much younger Archie inset over Nash's picture. 'I went to see him when I had your car on Monday…' She pushed herself slowly to her feet. She'd thought he was an old-time gardener from the estate. She'd thought Nash was… 'Lecture? What lecture?'

Vera obliged. '"Dr Nash Gallagher, grandson of Archer Baldwin, former owner of Summerville Hall, is returning to Maybridge today to give a guest lecture to students in the Biological and Environmental

Sciences School. Dr Gallagher has spent the last five years in South America, collecting and cataloguing new plant species, a number of which bear his name…'' da dee da dee da… Oh, listen to this. "A reliable source at the university confirmed earlier this week that Dr Gallagher is to be offered the new Chair in Botany, recently endowed by an unnamed benefactor…'' Whew. Did you know that, Stacey?'

'No.' Stacey took the paper from her. She'd hoped Dee was mistaken, but it was all there in black and white. 'I didn't know that. He's been lying to me.'

'Oh, now, Stacey…' Dee began.

'All right, I'll put it another way. He hasn't been telling me the truth. Even last night…' Even when he'd told her about his family, he hadn't told her the real truth. That it had all been about *money*.

No wonder Dee didn't know whether to laugh or cry.

Well, she knew. She'd cry. But not before she found him and told him exactly what she thought of him. She realised that Vera and Dee were staring at her. 'I'm going to get dressed now and go to the university,' she said quietly.

'Do you think that's wise?' Dee said quickly.

'I couldn't say. But I'm doing it anyway. Will you drive me or shall I call a taxi?' Well, she still had his phone. She might just use it to beat him to a bloody pulp. How dared he lie to her?

'I'll drive you. Who knows? I might be able to stop you making a complete fool of yourself.'

'It beats letting Nash Gallagher do it.'

'I'm sure he'll have a perfectly good reason for not telling you.'

'Really? Like what?' And she swung round briskly on her crutches just as a kitten skittered from beneath the table. It was the kitten or her. No contest.

'Stacey...sweetheart.' She opened her eyes and saw Nash leaning over her. For a moment she felt a warm glow of pleasure. 'What happened?'

He happened. That was what. And her quick joy at seeing him evaporated like a wisp of mist on a summer's morning. Insubstantial, lacking any staying power. 'Didn't Dee tell you?'

'She had to fetch the girls from school. She just said you had another fall.'

'That about sums it up. It was something of a repeat performance. Once again, I was in such a hurry to find you that I didn't see the danger until it was too late.'

'Find me? Why? You knew I was coming back.'

'Yes, but what I had to say wouldn't wait. I was in a hurry to find you because I was intent on bloody murder. It must have been your lucky day because I tripped over a kitten and banged my head. And this time they won't let me home, so you're safe. For now.'

'Don't move,' he said, as she tried to sit up. His hand, light as a thistle on her shoulder, was enough to keep her pinned to the pillow. Or it might have been the fact that she was as weak as that little kitten.

It didn't matter. She still had the use of the mouth.

'You're a rat, Nash. I trusted you. I took you at face value and loved you and you abused that trust. Why did you lie to me?' He opened his mouth, but she wasn't going to put up with any excuses. 'I saw the paper, so you'd better make it good.'

Nash could have said he'd never lied, that she just hadn't believed him when he'd told the truth. But that would have been fudging it. He'd hidden the truth from her and they both knew it.

'I'm sorry. Truly. At first it didn't seem important. Then, when it was, I wanted to be sure that it was me you wanted...not some mythical Baldwin millions.'

'That's despicable.'

'Yes, it is. But my father married my mother because of her money. He needed a start in business and that's how he got it.'

'And you thought I might do the same?' She couldn't believe her ears. Then, suddenly it all clicked into place. 'Because of Dee's matchmaking efforts with poor Lawrence? You think I'd marry a man who'd give me those ghastly forced roses?'

'You seemed pleased enough with them.' She gave him a look that suggested he was crazy and he lifted his shoulders in an awkward shrug. 'I'm sorry, Stacey. But until I met you I didn't have any notion of unconditional love.'

'Not even from Archie?'

'When I was small, I suppose. But even Archie used me in the end, as a weapon to hurt my mother.

He was still playing games with the garden centre. Trying to use it to get me to stay here.'

'And will you? Stay?'

'There's no money, Stacey. Archie gave it all away except the garden centre.' Then he pulled a face. 'Well, he might have kept the odd million tucked away in case he needed to endow a university chair. Still pulling strings, you see.'

'And will you do what he wants? Stay?'

'University professors don't earn that much, Stacey. I couldn't give you—'

'Oh, go away, Nash.' She was so tired, so hurt he thought it would make a difference, that she closed her eyes to shut him out. 'Just go away and grow up.' And when she opened her eyes again, he'd gone. But whether he grew up, she didn't know, because he didn't come back.

She was in hospital for a week, and after that Dee insisted she stay with her. Then, when she was feeling stronger, they all went away for a week to a cottage Dee rented in Dorset. Her sister was determinedly cheerful and kind, even forcing herself to say nice things about Cecile Latour and how good she'd been for Lawrence, quickly shushing the girls when they chattered eagerly about seeing Nash when they got home, wishing he could have come on holiday with them.

It was a distraction of sorts. And the rest and fresh air repaired her body, even if her spirits lagged.

'Home tomorrow. What'll you do?' Dee dropped into the chair beside her. 'Any ideas?'

Stacey sighed, stopped wishing that she hadn't been quite so hard on Nash. He'd only been trying to protect himself and he'd been good to her.

But life went on. It was time to brush off the life plan and get on with it. And, thinking of plans... 'Actually, Dee, I need a business plan. Have you any idea what that is?'

'Well, you need to have some way of raising capital.'

'I've got the house. I could raise money on that.'

'And you could lose it if the business goes wrong.'

'I know. But if I don't reach for the moon—' she stopped, remembering the night she and Nash had sat together in the garden '—how will I get the stars?'

Dee frowned. 'Bette Davis, *Now Voyager*,' she said. 'But I don't think it goes quite like that.'

'It doesn't. But it's near enough. Can I use your phone?' Dee handed it over. She dialled in Nash's number but it was switched off and she got his messaging service. 'Nash, this is Stacey. I'm ringing to tell you that I think three weeks is more than enough time for any man to grow up. I'll be home tomorrow and, if I'm right, I'll see you then.' When she handed the phone back, Dee was smiling. 'That's part of a different plan,' she said. 'Now, to business.'

It was one thing to call him long distance and leave a message. Another to be a mile from home with your heart beating a tattoo. Impatient to be home. Afraid that he wouldn't be there.

They turned into the lane. The house seemed to smile at them, welcoming them home. But there was no sign of Nash, or his motorbike.

Dee stopped and helped Stacey out and for a moment she stared at the house, not quite believing her eyes. 'It's been painted,' she said, stupidly.

'Looks good, doesn't it?'

'But...' Vera opened the front door. 'I don't understand. Who did this?' Oh, her heart was begging for it to be Nash. But surely this was too much for one man.

'Shall we go inside?' Dee urged. Clover and Rosie had already raced in to check out the kittens.

'What's been going on, Vera?' she demanded. 'Who did this?'

'Weren't they supposed to?' she asked, all innocence. 'They had a letter. Something about compensation for the accident.' She shrugged. 'They did the dining room, too. And put in a shower. I kept an eye on them,' she said, a touch affronted. 'I thought you'd be pleased.'

'I am, but I told Nash...' Archie owned the wall. Any compensation would have had to come from him. Her heart sank. This was it. As far as Nash was prepared to commit.

'Why don't you go and lie down?' Dee suggested. 'You must be tired. I'll take the girls home with me, if you like; Ingrid can give them their tea and I'll bring them back tomorrow.'

Stacey hadn't realised how empty the place would

seem. How miserable she would be. How sure she'd been that he would be there, waiting for her. Some hopes. He was probably halfway up the Amazon by now. She was certainly no fit company for her children. 'Yes. Thanks, Dee. That'd be great.'

Vera patted her arm. 'I'll be next door if you need anything.' Then, 'Can you manage the stairs?'

She nodded. 'No problem.' But Vera waited until she made the landing safely. Dee gathered up the children. The car started, drove away. And then there was just silence.

With a long shuddering sigh, she opened the bedroom door. The room was dim and she crossed slowly to the window to draw back the curtains.

Someone had started to cut the grass. She frowned. They'd made a bit of a mess of it; it had been cut here and there, leaving…a message. A message spelled out by the daisies.

STACEY—I LOVE YOU—WILL YOU MARRY ME?

Her hand flew to her mouth, her eyes filled with tears and yet she was laughing. Oh, yes. Oh, yes, please. And she flung open the window and shouted it out. 'Yes, Nash! Yes, please!' Nothing. She'd expected him to pop up over the new garden wall—although, come to think of it, there was a gate—'Nash, where are you?' she yelled. 'I want you! Now!'

'You've got me, sweetheart.' She swung around and there he was, standing in the doorway.

'Oh, come here! I've missed you so much! Why did you stay away?'

He obeyed without hesitation. Crossing the room in a few short strides to take her hand. 'You said not to come back until I grew up. Actually, it didn't take three weeks. It took about three minutes. But I thought I'd get the house sorted for you before I asked the big question. Just in case you said no.'

'Idiot,' she said, as he put his arms about her.

'Yeah,' he said. 'But I must have done something right. Look what I got.' And he kissed her. Slowly. Like a man with all the time in the world. Then, after a long time, he raised his head, regarded her with glittering eyes. 'You've got something, too,' he said, huskily.

'Yeah,' she said, and grinned. 'I noticed.'

But he produced a small box from his pocket. Opened it. The diamond solitaire was not just 'something'. It was stunning. 'Nash…I didn't…you didn't…'

'I know, darling. But there's a time for daisies and a time for diamonds. Will you marry me, Stacey?'

Her answer left him in no doubt.

The peaches were full and ripe and Nash lifted Clover to pick the first one. Then Primrose. Then it was the turn of her darling boy, with his skin like sunshine and hair the colour of clotted cream. He'd been named Archer, for his great-grandfather, but the girls had persisted in calling him Froggy until the name stuck.

Violet lay in her buggy, too young for peaches.

Stacey stroked her soft cheek and glanced around at her nursery. Babies and flowers, all were thriving.

Nash watched her, taking joy in the bloom of her contentment. 'Are you going to pick a peach, Nash?' Rosie asked him.

'No, sweetheart. Mummy and I will have ours later.' And, over the children's heads, their gazes met and held with a promise that, like daisies, went on growing year after year. And, like diamonds, was for ever.

NEARLYWEDS

Almost at the altar— will these *nearly*weds become *newly*weds?

Harlequin Romance® is delighted to invite you to some special weddings! Yet these are no ordinary weddings. Our beautiful brides and gorgeous grooms only *nearly* make it to the altar—before fate intervenes.

But the story doesn't end there....
Find out what happens in these tantalizingly emotional novels!

Authors to look out for include:

Leigh Michaels—The Bridal Swap
Liz Fielding—His Runaway Bride
Janelle Denison—The Wedding Secret
Renee Roszel—Finally a Groom
Caroline Anderson—The Impetuous Bride

Available wherever Harlequin books are sold.

HARLEQUIN®
Makes any time special ™

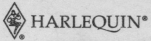

HARLEQUIN®

makes any time special—online...

your romantic escapes

● Indulgences

♥ Monthly guides to indulging yourself, such as:
  ★ Tub Time: A guide for bathing beauties
  ★ Magic Massages: A treat for tired feet

● Horoscopes

♥ Find your daily Passionscope, weekly Lovescopes and Erotiscopes

♥ Try our compatibility game

● Reel Love

♥ Read all the latest romantic movie reviews

● Royal Romance

♥ Get the latest scoop on your favorite royal romances

● Romantic Travel

♥ For the most romantic destinations, hotels and travel activities

Harlequin truly does make any time special. . . . This year we are celebrating weddings in style!

A Walk Down the Aisle
WEDDING CELEBRATION

To help us celebrate, we want you to tell us how wearing the Harlequin wedding gown will make your wedding day special. As the grand prize, Harlequin will offer one lucky bride the chance to **"Walk Down the Aisle" in the Harlequin wedding gown!**

There's more...

For her honeymoon, she and her groom will spend five nights at the **Hyatt Regency Maui.** As part of this five-night honeymoon at the hotel renowned for its romantic attractions, the couple will enjoy a candlelit dinner for two in Swan Court, a sunset sail on the hotel's catamaran, and duet spa treatments.

A HYATT RESORT AND SPA

MAUI *the Magic Isles*™
Maui • Molokai • Lanai

To enter, please write, in, 250 words or less, how wearing the Harlequin wedding gown will make your wedding day special. The entry will be judged based on its emotionally compelling nature, its originality and creativity, and its sincerity. This contest is open to Canadian and U.S. residents only and to those who are 18 years of age and older. There is no purchase necessary to enter. Void where prohibited. See further contest rules attached. Please send your entry to:

Walk Down the Aisle Contest

In Canada	In U.S.A.
P.O. Box 637	P.O. Box 9076
Fort Erie, Ontario	3010 Walden Ave.
L2A 5X3	Buffalo, NY 14269-9076

You can also enter by visiting www.eHarlequin.com

Win the Harlequin wedding gown and the vacation of a lifetime!
The deadline for entries is October 1, 2001.

HARLEQUIN®
Makes any time special ®

1. To enter, follow directions published in the offer to which you are responding. Contest begins April 2, 2001, and ends on October 1, 2001. Method of entry may vary. Mailed entries must be postmarked by October 1, 2001, and received by October 8, 2001.

2. Contest entry may be, at times, presented via the Internet, but will be restricted solely to residents of certain geographic areas that are disclosed on the Web site. To enter via the Internet, if permissible, access the Harlequin Web site (www.eHarlequin.com) and follow the directions displayed online. Online entries must be received by 11:59 p.m. E.S.T. on October 1, 2001.

   In lieu of submitting an entry online, enter by mail by hand-printing (or typing) on an 8½" x 11" plain piece of paper, your name, address (including zip code), Contest number/name and in 250 words or fewer, why winning a Harlequin wedding dress would make your wedding day special. Mail via first-class mail to: Harlequin Walk Down the Aisle Contest 1197, (in the U.S.) P.O. Box 9076, 3010 Walden Avenue, Buffalo, NY 14269-9076, (in Canada) P.O. Box 637, Fort Erie, Ontario L2A 5X3, Canada.

   Limit one entry per person, household address and e-mail address. Online and/or mailed entries received from persons residing in geographic areas in which Internet entry is not permissible will be disqualified.

3. Contests will be judged by a panel of members of the Harlequin editorial, marketing and public relations staff based on the following criteria:

   - Originality and Creativity—50%
   - Emotionally Compelling—25%
   - Sincerity—25%

   In the event of a tie, duplicate prizes will be awarded. Decisions of the judges are final.

4. All entries become the property of Torstar Corp. and will not be returned. No responsibility is assumed for lost, late, illegible, incomplete, inaccurate, nondelivered or misdirected mail or misdirected e-mail, for technical, hardware or software failures of any kind, lost or unavailable network connections, or failed, incomplete, garbled or delayed computer transmission or any human error which may occur in the receipt or processing of the entries in this Contest.

5. Contest open only to residents of the U.S. (except Puerto Rico) and Canada, who are 18 years of age or older, and is void wherever prohibited by law; all applicable laws and regulations apply. Any litigation within the Province of Quebec respecting the conduct or organization of a publicity contest may be submitted to the Régie des alcools, des courses et des jeux for a ruling. Any litigation respecting the awarding of a prize may be submitted to the Régie des alcools, des courses et des jeux only for the purpose of helping the parties reach a settlement. Employees and immediate family members of Torstar Corp. and D. L. Blair, Inc., their affiliates, subsidiaries and all other agencies, entities and persons connected with the use, marketing or conduct of this Contest are not eligible to enter. Taxes on prizes are the sole responsibility of winners. Acceptance of any prize offered constitutes permission to use winner's name, photograph or other likeness for the purposes of advertising, trade and promotion on behalf of Torstar Corp., its affiliates and subsidiaries without further compensation to the winner, unless prohibited by law.

6. Winners will be determined no later than November 15, 2001, and will be notified by mail. Winners will be required to sign and return an Affidavit of Eligibility form within 15 days after winner notification. Noncompliance within that time period may result in disqualification and an alternative winner may be selected. Winners of trip must execute a Release of Liability prior to ticketing and must possess required travel documents (e.g. passport, photo ID) where applicable. Trip must be completed by November 2002. No substitution of prize permitted by winner. Torstar Corp. and D. L. Blair, Inc., their parents, affiliates, and subsidiaries are not responsible for errors in printing or electronic presentation of Contest, entries and/or game pieces. In the event of printing or other errors which may result in unintended prize values or duplication of prizes, all affected game pieces or entries shall be null and void. If for any reason the Internet portion of the Contest is not capable of running as planned, including infection by computer virus, bugs, tampering, unauthorized intervention, fraud, technical failures, or any other causes beyond the control of Torstar Corp. which corrupt or affect the administration, secrecy, fairness, integrity or proper conduct of the Contest, Torstar Corp. reserves the right, at its sole discretion, to disqualify any individual who tampers with the entry process and to cancel, terminate, modify or suspend the Contest or the Internet portion thereof. In the event of a dispute regarding an online entry, the entry will be deemed submitted by the authorized holder of the e-mail account submitted at the time of entry. Authorized account holder is defined as the natural person who is assigned to an e-mail address by an Internet access provider, online service provider or other organization that is responsible for arranging e-mail address for the domain associated with the submitted e-mail address. **Purchase or acceptance of a product offer does not improve your chances of winning.**

7. Prizes: (1) Grand Prize—A Harlequin wedding dress (approximate retail value: $3,500) and a 5-night/6-day honeymoon trip to Maui, HI, including round-trip air transportation provided by Maui Visitors Bureau from Los Angeles International Airport (winner is responsible for transportation to and from Los Angeles International Airport) and a Harlequin Romance Package, including hotel accomodations (double occupancy) at the Hyatt Regency Maui Resort and Spa, dinner for (2) two at Swan Court, a sunset sail on Kiele V and a spa treatment for the winner (approximate retail value: $4,000); (5) Five runner-up prizes of a $1000 gift certificate to selected retail outlets to be determined by Sponsor (retail value $1000 ea.). Prizes consist of only those items listed as part of the prize. Limit one prize per person. All prizes are valued in U.S. currency.

8. For a list of winners (available after December 17, 2001) send a self-addressed, stamped envelope to: Harlequin Walk Down the Aisle Contest 1197 Winners, P.O. Box 4200 Blair, NE 68009-4200 or you may access the www.eHarlequin.com Web site through January 15, 2002.

Contest sponsored by Torstar Corp., P.O. Box 9042, Buffalo, NY 14269-9042, U.S.A.

PHWDACONT2

LONG, TALL TEXANS

EMMETT, REGAN & BURKE

New York Times
extended list bestselling author

Diana PALMER

returns to Jacobsville, Texas, in this special
collection featuring rugged heroes, spirited
heroines and passionate love stories told
in her own inimitable way!

Coming in May 2001 only from Silhouette Books!

Silhouette®
Where love comes alive™